AN ALIEN HEAT

AN ALIEN HEAT

Volume One of a Trilogy
"The Dancers at the End of Time"

Michael Moorcock

Harper & Row, Publishers
New York, Evanston, San Francisco, London

For Nik Turner, Dave Brock, Bob Calvert,
DikMik, Del Dettmar, Terry Ollis, Simon King and
Lemmy of Hawkwind.

The silver lips of lilies virginal,
The full deep bosom of the enchanted rose
Please less than flowers glass-hid from frosts and snows
For whom an alien heat makes festival.

THEODORE WRATISLAW
Hothouse Flowers
1896

CONTENTS

PROLOGUE

THE cycle of the Earth (indeed, the universe, if the truth had been known) was nearing its end and the human race had at last ceased to take itself seriously. Having inherited millennia of scientific and technological knowledge it used this knowledge to indulge its richest fantasies, to play immense imaginative games, to relax and create beautiful monstrosities. After all, there was little else left to do. An earlier age might have been horrified at what it would have judged a waste of resources, an appalling extravagance in the uses to which materials and energies were put. An earlier age would have seen the inhabitants of this world as 'decadent' or 'amoral', to say the least. But even if these inhabitants were not conscious of the fact that they lived at the end of time some unconscious knowledge informed their attitudes and made them lose interest in ideals, creeds, philosophies and the conflicts to which such things give rise. They found pleasure in paradox, aesthetics and baroque wit; if they had a philosophy, then it was a philosophy of taste, of sensuality. Most of the old emotions had atrophied, meant little to them. They had rivalry without jealousy, affection without lust, malice without rage, kindness without pity. Their schemes—often grandiose and perverse —were pursued without obsession and left uncompleted without regret, for death was rare and life might cease only when Earth herself died.

Yet this particular story is about an obsession which overtook one of these people, much to his own astonishment. And because he was overtaken by an obsession that is why we have a story to tell. It is probably the last story in the annals of the human race and, as it happens, it is not dissimilar to that which many believe is the first.

What follows, then, is the story of Jherek Carnelian, who did not know the meaning of morality, and Mrs Amelia Underwood, who knew everything about it.

CHAPTER ONE

A CONVERSATION WITH THE IRON ORCHID

DRESSED in various shades of light brown, the Iron Orchid and her son sat upon a cream-coloured beach of crushed bone. Some distance off a white sea sparkled and whispered. It was the afternoon.

Between the Iron Orchid and her son, Jherek Carnelian, lay the remains of a lunch. Spread on a cloth of plain damask were ivory plates contaning pale fish, potatoes, meringue, vanilla ice-cream and, glaring rather dramatically, from the centre of it all, a lemon.

The Iron Orchid smiled with her amber lips and, reaching for an oyster, asked: 'How do you mean, my love, "virtuous"?' Her perfect hand, powdered the very lightest shade of gold, hovered for a second over the oyster and then withdrew. She used the hand, instead, to cover a small yawn.

Her son stretched on his soft pillows. He, too, felt tired after the exertions of eating, but dutifully he continued with the subject. 'I'm not thoroughly sure what it means. As you know, most devastating of minerals, most enchanting of flowers, I have studied the language of the time quite extensively. I must possess every tape that still exists. It provides considerable amusement. But I cannot understand every nuance. I found the word in a dictionary and the dictionary told me it meant acting with "moral rectitude" or in conformity with "moral laws"—"good, just, righteous". Bewildering!'

He did take an oyster. He slid it into his mouth. He rolled it down his throat. It had been the Iron Orchid who had discovered oysters and he had been delighted when she suggested they meet on this beach and eat them. She had made some champagne to go with them, but they had both agreed that they did not care for it and had cheerfully returned it to its component atoms.

'However,' he continued, 'I should like to try it for a bit. It is supposed to involve "self-denial" '—he forestalled her question—'which means doing nothing pleasurable.'

'But *everything*, body of velvet, bones of steel, is pleasurable!'

'True—and there lies our paradox! You see the ancients, mother, divided their sensations into different groupings—categories of sensations, some of which they did not find pleasurable, it seems. Or they did find them pleasurable and therefore were displeased! Oh, dearest Iron Orchid, I can see you are ready to dismiss the whole thing. And I despair, often, of puzzling out the answer. Why was one thing considered worth pursuing and another not? But,' his handsome lips curved in a smile, 'I shall settle the problem in one way or another, sooner or later.' And he closed his heavy lids.

'Oh, Carnelian!'

She laughed softly and affectionately and stretched across the cloth to slip her slender hands into his loose robe and stroke his warmth and his blood.

'Oh, my dear! How swift you are! How ripe and rich you are today!'

And he drew himself to his feet and he stepped over the cloth and he laid his tall body down upon her and he kissed her slowly.

And the sea sighed.

When they awoke, still in each other's arms, it was morning, though no night had passed. For their own pleasure someone had doubtless been engaged in rearranging time. It was not important.

Jherek noticed that the sea had turned a deep pink, almost a cerise, and was clashing dreadfully with the beach, while on the horizon behind him he saw that two palms and a cliff had disappeared altogether. In their place stood a silver pagoda, about twelve storeys high and glittering in the morning sun.

Jherek looked to his left and was pleased to see that his aircar (resembling a steam locomotive of the early 20th century, but of about half the size, in gold, ebony and rubies) was still where they had left it.

He looked again at the pagoda, craning his neck, for his mother still relaxed with her head against his shoulder. His mother, too, turned to look as a winged figure left the roof of the pagoda and flew crazily away towards the east, swerving and dipping, circling back, narrowly missing the sharp edge of the pagoda's crest, and at last disappearing.

'Oh,' said the Iron Orchid getting to her feet. 'It is the Duke of Queens and his wings. Why will he insist that they are successful?' She waved a vague hand at the departed duke. 'Good-bye. Playing one of his solitary games, again, I suppose.' She looked down at the remains of the lunch and made a face. 'I must clear this away.' With a wave of the ring on her left hand she disseminated the lunch and watched the dust drift away on the air. 'Will you be going there, this evening? To his party?' She moved her slender arm, heavy with brown brocade, and touched her forehead with her fingertips.

'I think so.' He disseminated his own pillows. 'I have a great liking for the Duke of Queens.'

His lips pursed a trifle, Jherek Carnelian pondered the pink sea. 'Even if I do not always appreciate his colour sense.'

He turned and walked over the crushed bone beach to his aircar. He clambered into the cabin.

'All aboard, my strong, my sweet, Iron Orchid!'

She chuckled and reached up to him.

From the footplate he reached down, seized her waist and swung her aboard.

'Off to Pasadena!'

He sounded his whistle.

'Shuffle on to Buffalo!'

Responding to the sonic signal, the little locomotive took magnificently to the air, shunting up the sky, with lovely, lime-coloured steam puffing from its smokestack and from beneath its wheels.

'Oh, they gave him his augurs at Racine-Virginia,' sang Jherek Carnelian, donning a scarlet and cloth-of-gold engineer's cap, 'saying steam-up, you're way behind time! It ain't '98, it's old '97. You got to get on down that old Nantucket line!'

The Iron Orchid settled back in her seat of plush and ermine (an exact reproduction, she understood, of the original) and watched her son with amusement as he opened the firedoor and shovelled in the huge black diamonds which he had made specially to go with the train and which, though of no particular use in fuelling the aircar, added aesthetic texture to the recreation.

'Where do you *find* all these old songs, Carnelian, my own?'

'I came across a cache of "platters",' he told her, wiping honest sweat from his face with a silk rag. The train swept rapidly over a sea and a range of mountains. 'A form of sound-storage of the same period as the original of this aircar. A million years old, at least, though there's some evidence that they, themselves, are reproductions of other originals. Kept in perfect condition by a succession of owners.'

He slammed the firedoor shut and discarded the platinum shovel, joining her upon the couch and staring down at the quaintly moulded countryside which Mistress Christia, the Everlasting Concubine, had begun to build a while ago and then abandoned.

It was not elegant. In fact it was something of a mess. Two-thirds of a hill, in the fashion of the 91st century post-Aryan landscapers, supported a snake-tree done after the Saturnian manner but left uncoloured; part of an 11th century Gothic ruin stood beside a strip of river of the Bengali Empire period. You could see why she had decided not to finish it, but it seemed to Jherek that it was a pity she had not bothered to disseminate it. Someone else would, of course, sooner or later.

'Carrie Joan,' he sang, 'she kept her boiler going. Carrie Joan, she filled it full of wine. Carrie Joan didn't stop her rowing. She had to get to Brooklyn by a quarter-past nine!'

He turned to the Iron Orchid.

'Do you like it? The quality of the platters isn't all it could be, but I think I've worked out all the words now.'

'Is that what you were doing last year?'

She raised her fine eyebrows. 'I heard the noises coming from your Hi-Rise.' She laughed. 'And I thought it was to do with sex.' She frowned. 'Or animals.' She smiled. 'Or both.'

The locomotive began to spiral down, hooting, towards Jherek's ranch. The ranch had taken the place of the Hi-Rise. A typical building of the 19th century, done in fiba-fome and thatch, each corner of its veranda roof was supported by a wooden Indian, some forty feet high. Each Indian had a magnificent pearl, twelve inches in diameter, in his turban, and a beard of real hair. The Indians were the only extravagant detail in the otherwise simple building.

The locomotive landed in the corral and Jherek, whose interest in the ancient world had, off and on, sustained itself for nearly two years, held out his hand to help the Iron Orchid disembark. For a moment she hesitated as she attempted to remember what she must do. Then she grasped his hand and jumped to the ground crying:

'Geronimo!'

Together they made for the house.

The surrounding landscape had been designed to fit in with the ranch. The sky contained a sunset, which silhouetted the purple hills, and the black pines, which topped them. On the other side was a range containing a herd of bison. Every few days there would emerge from a cunningly hidden opening in the ground a group

4

of mechanical 7th cavalrymen who would whoop and shout and ride round and round the bison shooting their arrows into the air before roping and branding the beasts. The bison had been specially grown from Jherek's own extensive gene-bank and didn't seem to care for the operation, although it should have been instinctive to them. The 7th cavalry, on the other hand, had been manufactured in his machine shop because he had a distaste for growing people (who were inclined to be bad-mannered when the time came for their dissemination).

'What a beautiful sunset,' said his mother, who had not visited him since the Hi-Rise days. 'Was the sun really as huge as that in those days?'

'Bigger,' he said, 'by all accounts. I toned it down rather, for this.'

She touched his arm. 'You were always inclined to be restrained. I like it.'

'Thank you.'

They went up the white winding staircase to the veranda, breathing in the delicious scent of magnolia which grew on the ground beside the basement section of the house. They crossed the veranda and Jherek manipulated a lever which, depressed, allowed the door to open so that they could enter the parlour—a single room occupying the whole of this floor. The remaining eight floors were given over to kitchens, bedrooms, cupboards and the like.

The parlour was a treasure house of 19th century reproductions, including a magnificent pot-bellied stove carved from a single oak and a flowering aspidistra which grew from the centre of the grass carpet and spread its rubbery branches over the best part of the room.

The Iron Orchid hovered beside the intricate lattice-work shape which Jherek had seen in an old holograph and reproduced in steel and chrome. It was like a huge egg standing on its end and it rose as high as the ceiling.

'And what is this, my life force?' she asked him.

'A spaceship,' he explained. 'They were constantly attempting to fly to the moon or striving to repel invasions from Mars. I'm not sure if they were successful, though of course there are no Martians these days. Some of their writers were inclined to tell rather tall tales, you know, doubtless with a view to entertaining their companions.'

'Whatever possessed them to *try!* Into *space!*'

She shuddered. People had lost the inclination to leave the Earth centuries ago.

Naturally, space-travellers called on the planet from time to time, but they were, as often as not, boring fellows with not much to offer. They were usually encouraged to leave as soon as possible or, if one should catch somebody's fancy, he would be retained in a collection.

Even Jherek had no impulse to time-travel, though time-travellers would arrive occasionally in his era. He could have travelled through time himself, if he had wished, and very briefly visited his beloved 19th century. But, like most people, he found that the real places were rather disappointing. It was much better to indulge in imaginative recreation of the periods or places. Nothing, therefore, would spoil the full indulgence of one's fancies, or the thrill of discovery as one unearthed some new piece of information and added it to the texture of one's reproduction.

A servo entered and bowed. The Iron Orchid handed it her clothes (as she had been instructed to do by Jherek—another custom of the time) and went to stretch her wonderful body under the aspidistra tree.

Jherek was pleased to note she was wearing breasts again and thus did not clash with her surroundings. Everything was in period. Even the servo wore a derby, an ulster, chaps and stout brogues and carried several meerschaum pipes in its steel teeth. At a sign from its master it rolled away.

Jherek went to sit with his back against the bole of the aspidistra. 'And now, lovely Iron Orchid, tell me what you have been doing.'

She looked up at him, her eyes shining. 'I've been making babies, dearest. Hundreds of them!' She giggled. 'I couldn't stop. Cherubs, mainly. I built a little aviary for them, too. And I made them trumpets to blow and harps to pluck and I composed the sweetest music you ever heard. And they played it!'

'I should like to hear it.'

'What a shame.' She was genuinely upset that she had not thought of him, her favourite, her only real son. 'I'm making microscopes now. And gardens, of course, to go with them. And tiny beasts. But perhaps I'll do the cherubs again some day. And you shall hear them, then.'

'If I am not being "virtuous",' he said archly.

'Ah, now I begin to understand the meaning. If you have an impulse to do something—you do the opposite. You want to be a man, so you become a woman. You wish to fly somewhere, so you go underground. You wish to drink, but instead you emit fluid. And so on. Yes, that's splendid. You'll set a fashion, mark my words. In a month, blood of my blood, *everyone* will be virtuous. And what shall we do then? Is there anything else? Tell me!'

'Yes. We could be "evil"—or "modest"—or "lazy"—or "poor"—or, oh, I don't know—"worthy". There's hundreds.'

'And you would tell us how to be it?'

'Well . . .' He frowned. 'I still have to work out exactly what's involved. But by that time I should know a little more.'

'We'll all be grateful to you. I remember when you taught us Lunar Cannibals. And Swimming. And—what was it—Flags?'

'I enjoyed Flags,' he said. 'Particularly when My Lady Charlotina made that delicious one which covered the whole of the western hemisphere. In metal cloth the thickness of an ant's web. Do you remember how we laughed when it fell on us?'

'Oh, yes!' She clapped her hands. 'Then Lord Jagged built a Flag Pole on which to fly it and the pole melted so we each made a Niagara to see who could do the biggest and used up every drop of water and had to make a whole new batch and you went round and round in a cloud raining on everyone, even on Mongrove. And Mongrove dug himself an underground Hell, with devils and everything, out of that book the time-traveller brought us, and he set fire to Bulio Himmler's "Bunkerworld 2" which he didn't know was right next door to him and Bulio was so upset he kept dropping atom bombs on Mongrove's Hell, not knowing that he was supplying Mongrove with all the heat he needed!'

They laughed heartily.

'Was it really three hundred years ago?' said Jherek nostalgically.

He plucked a leaf from the aspidistra and reflectively began to chew it. A little blue juice ran down his beige chin.

'I sometimes think,' he continued, 'that I haven't known a better sequence of events. It seemed to go on and on, one thing leading neatly to another. Mongrove's Hell, you know, also ruined my menagerie, except for one creature that escaped and broke most of his devils. Everything went up, in my menagerie, otherwise. Because of Himmler, really. Or because of Lady Charlotina. Who's to say?'

He discarded the leaf.

'It's strange,' he said. 'I haven't kept a menagerie since. I mean,

7

'almost everyone has some sort of menagerie, even you, Iron Orchid.'

'Mine is so *small*. Compare it with the Everlasting Concubine's, even.'

'You've three Napoleons. She has none.'

'True. But I'm honestly not sure whether any one of them is genuine.'

'It is hard to tell,' he agreed.

'And she does have an absolutely genuine Attila the Hun. The trouble she went to, too, to make that particular trade. But he's such a bore.'

'I think that's why I stopped collecting,' he said. 'The genuine items are often less interesting than the fakes.'

'It's usually the case, fruit of my loins.' She sank into the grass again. This last reference was not to the literal truth. In fact, as Jherek remembered, his mother had been some sort of male anthropoid at the actual moment of his birth and had forgotten all about him until, by accident, six months later she came upon the incubator in the jungle she had built. He had still been nursed as a new-born baby by the incubator. But she had kept him. He was glad of that. So few human beings, as such, were born these days.

Perhaps that was why, being a natural born baby, as it were, he felt such an affinity with the past, thought Jherek. Many of the time-travellers—even some of the space-travellers—had been children, too.

He did get on well with some of the people who had chosen to live outside the menageries and adopt the ways of this society.

Pereg Tralo, for instance, who had ruled the world in the 30th century simply because he had been the last person to be born out of an actual womb! A splendid, witty companion. And Clare Cyrato, the singer from the 500th—a peculiar freak, due to some experiment of her mother's, she too had entered life as a baby. Babies, children, adolescents—everything!

It was an experience he had not regretted. What experience could be regretted? And he had been the darling of all his mother's friends. His novelty lasted well into his teens. With delight they had watched him *grow!* Everyone envied him. Everyone envied the Iron Orchid, though for a while she had distinctly tired of him and gone away to live in the middle of a mountain. Everyone envied him, that is, except Mongrove (who would certainly not have admitted it, anyway) and Werther de Goethe, who had also been born a baby.

8

Werther, of course, had been a trial and had not enjoyed himself nearly so much. Even though he no longer had six arms, he still felt a certain amount of resentment about the way he had been altered, never having the same limbs or the same head, even, from one day to the next.

Jherek noticed that his mother had fallen asleep again. She only had to lie down for a moment and she was dreaming. It was a habit she had always encouraged in herself, for she thought up many of her best new ideas in dreams.

Jherek hardly dreamed at all.

If he had, he supposed he would not have to seek out old tapes and platters to read, watch or hear.

Still, he was acknowledged as being one of the very best recreators, even if his originality would not equal either his mother's or that of the Duke of Queens. Privately Jherek felt that the Duke of Queens lost on aesthetic sensibility what he made up for in invention.

Jherek remembered that both he and the Iron Orchid were invited to the Duke's that evening. He had not been to a party for some time and was determined to wear something stunning.

He considered what to put on. He would stick to the 19th century, of course, for he believed very much in consistency of style. And it must be nothing fanciful. It must be spare. It must be a clean, quiet image, striking and absolutely without a personal touch. A personal touch would, again, mar the effect. The choice became obvious.

He would wear full evening dress, an opera hat and an opera cloak.

And, he thought with a self-satisfied smile, he would have the whole thing in a low-keyed combination of russet orange and midnight blue. With a carnation, naturally, at the throat.

CHAPTER TWO

A SOIRÉE AT THE DUKE OF QUEENS

A FEW million years ago, perhaps less (for time was terribly difficult to keep track of), there had flourished as a province of legendary New York City a magnificent district known as the Queen's. It was here that some New York king's escort had established her summer residence, building a vast palace and gardens and inviting from all over the world the most talented and the most amusing people to share the summer months with her. To the Queen's court flocked great painters, writers, composers, sculptors, craftsmen and wits, to display their new creations, to perform plays, dances and operas, to gossip, to entertain their queen (who had probably been the mythical Queen Eleanor of the Red Veldt), their patron.

Although in the meantime a few continents had drowned and others emerged, while various land masses had joined together and some had divided, there had been little doubt in the mind of Liam Ty Pam Caesar Lloyd George Zatopek Finsbury Ronnie Michelangelo Yurio Iopu 4578 Rew United that he had found the site of the original court and established his own residence there and was thus able to style himself, reasonably enough, the Duke of Queens. One of the few permanent landmarks of the world was his statue of the Queen of the Red Veldt herself, stretching half a mile into the sky and covering an area of some six miles, showing the heroic queen in her cadillac (or chariot) drawn by six dragons, with her oddly curved spear in one hand, her square shield on her other arm and with her bizarre helmet upon her head, looking splendidly heroic as she must have done when she led her victorious armies against the might of the United Nations, that grandiose and ambitious alliance which had, in the legends, once sought to dominate the entire planet. So long had the statue stood in the grounds of the Duke's residence that few really ever noticed it, for the residence itself changed frequently and the Duke of Queens often managed to astonish everyone with the originality and scope of his invention.

As Jherek Carnelian and his mother, the Iron Orchid, approached, the first thing they saw was the statue, but almost immediately they took note of the house which the Duke must have erected especially for this evening's party.

'Oh!' breathed the Iron Orchid, peering out from the cabin of the locomotive and shielding her eyes against the light, 'How clever he is! How delightful!'

Jherek pretended to be unimpressed as he joined her on the footplate, his opera cloak swirling.

'It's pretty,' he said, 'and striking, of course. The Duke of Queens is always striking.'

Clad in poppies, marigolds and cornflowers from throat to ankle, the Iron Orchid turned with a smile and wagged a finger at him. 'Come now, my dear. Admit that it is magnificent.'

'I have admitted that it is striking. It is striking.'

'It is magnificent!'

His disdain melted before her enthusiasm. He laughed. 'Very well, lushest of blooms, it is *magnificent!* Without parallel! Gorgeous! Breathtaking! A work of genius!'

'And you will tell him so, my ghost?' Her eyes were sardonic. 'Will you tell him?'

He bowed. 'I will.'

'Splendid. And then, you see, we shall enjoy the party so much more.'

Of course, there was no doubting the Duke's ingenuity but as usual, thought Jherek, he had overdone everything. The sky had been coloured a lurid purple as a background and in it swirled the remaining planets of the Solar System—Mars as a great ruby, Venus as an emerald, Herod as a diamond, and so on—thirty in all.

The residence itself was a reproduction of the Great Fire of Africa. There were a number of separate buildings, each in the shape of some famous city of the time, blazing merrily away. Durban, Kilwa-Kivinje, Yola, Timbuctoo and others all burned, yet each detailed building, which was certain to be in perfect scale, was sculpted from water and the water was brightly (garishly, in Jherek's opinion) coloured, as were the flames. There were flames of every conceivable, flickering shade. And among the flames and the water wandered the guests who had already arrived. Naturally there was no heat to the fire—or barely any—for the Duke of Queens had no intention of burning his guests to death. In a way, Jherek thought, that was why the residence seemed to him to lack any real creative force.

But then he was inclined to take such matters too seriously—everyone told him of that.

The locomotive landed just outside Smithsmith, whose towers and terraces would crumble as if in a blaze and then swiftly reform themselves before the water fell on anybody. People shouted with delight and giggled in surprise. Smithsmith seemed at present the most popular attraction in the residence. Food and beverages, mainly 28th century African, were laid about everywhere and people wandered from table to table sampling them.

Dismounting from the footplate and absently offering his hand to his mother (whose 'Geronimo' was *sotto voce* because she was becoming bored with the ritual) Jherek noticed many people he knew and a few whom he did not. Some of those he did not know were plainly from menageries, probably all time-travellers. He could tell by the awkward way in which they stood, either conversing or keeping to themselves, either amused or unhappy. Jherek saw a time-traveller he did recognise. Li Pao, clad in his usual blue overalls, was casting a disapproving eye over Smithsmith.

Jherek and the Iron Orchid approached him.

'Good evening, Li Pao,' said the Iron Orchid. She kissed him on his lovely, round yellow face. 'You're evidently critical of Smithsmith. Is it the usual? Lack of authenticity? You're from the 28th century, aren't you?'

'27th,' said Li Pao, 'but I don't imagine things would have changed that much. Ah, you bourgeois individualists—you're so bad at it. That's always been my main contention.'

'You could be a better "bourgeois individualist" if you wanted to be, eh?' Another menagerie member approached. He was dressed in the long, silver skirts of the 32nd century whipperman. 'You're always quibbling over details, Li Pao.'

Li Pao sighed. 'I know. I'm boring. But there it is.'

'It's why we love you,' said the Iron Orchid, kissing him again and then waving her hand to her dear friend Gaf the Horse in Tears who had looked up from her conversation with Sweet Orb Mace (whom some thought might be Jherek's father) and smiled at the Iron Orchid, motioning her to join them. The Iron Orchid drifted away.

'And it's why we won't listen to you time-travellers,' said Jherek. 'You can be so dreadfully pedantic. This detail isn't right—that one's

12

out of period—and so on. It spoils everyone's pleasure. You must admit, Li Pao, that you are a trifle literal minded.'

'That was the strength of our Republic,' said Li Pao, sipping his wine. 'That was why it lasted fifty thousand years.'

'Off and on,' said the 32nd century whipperman.

'More on than off,' said Li Pao.

'Well, it depends what you call a republic,' said the whipperman.

They were at it again. Jherek Carnelian smoothed himself off and saw Mongrove, the bitter giant, all overblown and unloved, who stood moping in the very centre of blazing Smithsmith as if he wished the buildings would really fall down on him and consume him. Jherek knew that Mongrove's whole persona was an affectation, but he had kept it so long that it was almost possible Mongrove had become the thing itself. But Mongrove was not really unloved. He was a favourite at parties—when he deigned to attend them. This must be his first in twenty years.

'How are you, Lord Mongrove?' Jherek asked, staring up at the giant's lugubrious face.

'The worse for seeing you, Jherek Carnelian. I have not forgotten all the slights, you know.'

'You would not be Mongrove if you had.'

'The turning of my feet into rats. You were only a boy, then.'

'Correct. The first slight.' Jherek bowed.

'The theft of my private poems.'

'True—and my publishing them.'

'Just so.' Mongrove nodded, continuing: 'The shifting of my lair and its environs from the North to the South pole.'

'You were confused.'

'Confused and angry with you, Jherek Carnelian. The list is endless. I know that I am your butt, your fool, your plaything. I know what you think of me.'

'I think well of you, Lord Mongrove.'

'You know me for what I am. A monster. A horror. A thing which does not deserve to live. And I hate you for that, Jherek Carnelian.'

'You love me for it, Mongrove. Admit it.'

A deep sigh, almost a windy bellow, escaped the giant's lips and tears fell from his eyes as he turned away. 'Do your worst, Jherek Carnelian. Do your worst to me.'

'If you insist, my darling Mongrove.'

Jherek smiled as he watched Mongrove plod deeper into the holocaust, his great shoulders slumped, his huge hands hanging heavily at his hips. Dressed all in black was Mongrove, with his skin, hair and eyes stained black, too. Jherek wondered if he and Mongrove would ever consummate their love for each other. Perhaps Mongrove had learned the secret of 'virtue'? Perhaps the giant deliberately sought the opposite of everything he really desired to think and do? Jherek felt he was beginning to understand. However, he didn't much like the idea of turning into another Mongrove. That would be an awful thing to do. It was the only thing which Mongrove would truly resent.

However, thought Jherek as he strolled on through the flames and the liquids, if *he* became Mongrove would not Mongrove then have an incentive to become something else? But would that new Mongrove be as delightful as the old? It was unlikely.

'Jherek, my delicious fancy! Here!'

Jherek turned with a crack of his russet cloak and saw Lord Jagged of Canaria, a mass of quilted yellow, his head barely visible in his puffy collar, signalling to be joined at a table of fruits.

'Lord Jagged.' Jherek embraced his friend. 'Well, cosy one, are your battles ended?'

'They are ended at last. It has been five years. But they are ended. And every little man dead, I fear.' Lord Jagged had invented a perfect facsimile of the Solar System and had played out every war on it he had ever heard of. Each soldier had been complete in every detail, though of sub-microscopic proportions. A tiny personality. The entire set had been built in a cube measuring just over two feet square. Lord Jagged yawned and for a moment his face disappeared altogether into his collar. 'Yes, I quite lost affection for them in the end. Silly things. And you, handsome Jherek, what do you do?'

'Nothing very ambitious. Reproductions of the ancient world. Have you seen my locomotive?'

'I don't even know the word!' Lord Jagged roared. 'Shall I see it now?'

'It's over there, somewhere,' said Jherek, pointing through a tumbling skyscraper. 'It can wait until you are nearer.'

'Your costume is admirable,' said Lord Jagged, fingering the cloak. 'I have always envied your taste, Jherek. Is this, too, something the ancients wore?'

'Exactly.'

'Exactly! Oh, your patience! Your care! Your *eye!*'

Jherek stretched his arms and looked about him, pleased by the compliment. 'It is fine,' he said, 'my eye.'

'But where is our host, the magnificent Duke of Queens, the inventor of all this excitement?'

Jherek knew that Lord Jagged shared his view of the Duke's taste. He shook his head. 'I haven't seen him. Perhaps in one of the other cities. Is there a main one?'

'I think not. It is possible, of course, that he has not yet arrived—or left already. You know how he loves to absent himself. Such a strong, *dramatic* sense.'

'And droll,' said Jherek, meeting his friend's eyes and smiling.

'Now, now,' said Lord Jagged. 'Let us, Jherek, *circulate*. Then, perhaps, we'll find our host and be able to compliment him to his face.'

Arm in arm they moved through the blazing city, crossed the lawns and entered Timbuctoo, whose slender oblongs, crowned by minarets, fell in upon each other, criss-crossed, nearly struck the ground and then sprang upright again, to be consumed by the flames afresh.

'Chrome,' Jherek heard Li Pao saying. 'They were chrome. Not silver and quartz and gold at all. To me, I'm afraid, that spoils the whole idea.'

Jherek chuckled. 'Do you know Li Pao? I suspect that he did not travel willingly through time. I suspect, my padded Jagged, that his comrades *sent* him off! I am learning "virtue", by the way.'

'And what is "virtue"?'

'I think it involves being like Mongrove.'

'Oh!' Lord Jagged rounded his lips in an ironic expression of dismay.

'I know. But you're familiar with my perfectionism.'

'Of its kind it is the sweetest.'

'I think you taught me that—when I was a boy.'

'I remember! I remember!' Lord Jagged sighed reminiscently.

'And I am grateful.'

'Nonsense. A boy needs a father. I was there.' The puffed sleeve stretched out and a pale hand emerged to touch Jherek lightly upon his carnation, to pluck a tiny petal from it and touch it so elegantly to the pale lips. 'I was there, my heart.'

'One day,' said Jherek, 'we must make love, Lord Jagged.'

'One day. When the mood comes upon us at the same time. Yes.'

Lord Jagged's lips smiled. 'I look forward to it. And how is your mother?'

'She is sleeping a great deal again.'

'Then we may expect something extraordinary from her soon.'

'I think so. She is here.'

Lord Jagged drew away from Jherek. 'Then I shall look for her. Farewell.'

'Good-bye, golden Lord Jagged.'

Jherek watched his friend disappear through an archway of fire which was there for a moment before the towers reformed.

It was true that Lord Jagged of Canaria had helped form his taste and was, perhaps, the kindest, most affectionate person in all the world. Yet there was a certain sadness about him which Jherek could never understand. Lord Jagged, it was sometimes said, had not been created in this age at all, but had been a time-traveller. Jherek had once put this to Lord Jagged but had met with an amused denial. Yet still Jherek was not sure. He wondered why, if Jagged were a time-traveller, he would wish to make a secret of it.

Jherek realised that he was frowning. He rearranged his expression and sauntered on through Timbuctoo. How dull the 28th century must have been. Odd that things could change so swiftly in the course of a few hundred years so that a century like the 19th could be full of richness and a century like the 28th could only offer the Great Fire of Africa. Still, it was all a matter of what happened to amuse the individual. He really must try to be less critical of the Duke of Queens.

A pride of lions appeared and prowled menacingly around Jherek, growling and sniffing. They were real. He wondered if the Duke of Queens had gone so far as to allow them all their instincts. But they lost interest in him and swaggered on. Their colours, predominantly blue and green, clashed as usual. Elsewhere Jherek heard people giggling in fear as the lions found them. Most people found such sensations gratifying. He wondered if his pursuit of virtue was making him bad-tempered. If so, he would swiftly become a bore and had best abandon the whole idea. He saw Mistress Christia, the Everlasting Concubine, lying on her back near the edge of the burning city and humping up and down with glad cries as O'Kala Incarnadine, who had turned himself into a gorilla for the occasion, enjoyed her. She saw Jherek and waved. 'Jherek!' she panted. 'I— would—*love*—to—see—— Oh, Kala, my love, that's enough. Do you mind?' But I want to talk to Jherek now.' The gorilla turned its head and saw Jherek and grinned at him.

'Hello, Jherek. I didn't realise,' said O'Kala Incarnadine. He got up, smoothing down his fur. 'Thank you, Mistress Christia.'

'Thank you, O'Kala. That was lovely.' She spoke vaguely as she concentrated on rearranging her skirts. 'How are you, Jherek. Can I serve?'

'Always, as you know. But I would rather chat.'

'So would I, to be frank. O'Kala has been a gorilla now for several weeks and I'm *constantly* bumping into him and I'm beginning to suspect that these meetings aren't accidental. Not that I mind, of course. But I'll admit that I'm thinking of going back to being a man again. And maybe a gorilla. Your mother was a gorilla for a while, wasn't she? How did she enjoy it?'

'I was too young to remember, Mistress Christia.'

'Of course you were!' She looked him over. 'A baby! I remember.'

'You would, my delicacy.'

'There is nothing to stop anyone *becoming* a child for a while. I wonder why more people don't do it?'

'The fashion never did catch on,' Jherek agreed, seizing her about the waist and kissing her neck and shoulders. She kissed him back. She really was one of the most perfect identity-creations in the world. No man could resist her. Whatever he felt like he had to kiss her and often had to make love to her. Even Mongrove. Even Werther de Goethe who, as a boy, had never enjoyed her.

'Have you seen Werther de Goethe?' Jherek asked.

'He *was* here, earlier,' said Mistress Christia looking about her. 'I saw him with Mongrove. They do like one another's company, don't they?'

'Mongrove learns from Werther, I think,' said Jherek. 'And Werther says that Mongrove is the only sane person in the whole world.'

'Perhaps it's true. What does "sane" mean?'

'I shan't tell you. I've had enough of defining difficult words and ideas today.'

'Oh, Jherek! What are you up to?'

'Very little. My interests have always tended towards the abstract. It makes me poor company and I am determined to improve.'

'You're lovely company, Jherek. Everyone loves you.'

'I know. And I intend to continue being loved. You know how

tiresome I'd become—like Li Pao—if I did nothing but talk and invented little.'

'Everyone loves Li Pao!'

'Of course. But I do not wish to be loved in the way Li Pao is loved.'

She offered him a glance of secret amusement.

'Is *that* how I'm loved?' he asked in horror.

'Not quite. But you *were* a child, Jherek. The questions you asked!'

'I'm mortified.' He was not. He realised that he did not really care. He laughed.

'You're right,' she said. 'Li Pao is a bore and even I find him tiresome occasionally. Have you heard that the Duke of Queens has a surprise for us?'

'Another.'

'Jherek—you are not generous to the Duke of Queens. And that isn't fair, for the Duke is a very generous host.'

'Yes, I know. What is the nature of this new surprise?'

'That, too, is a surprise.' High above little African flying machines began to bomb the city. Bright lights burst everywhere and screamed as they burst. 'Oh, that's how it started!' exclaimed Mistress Christia. 'He's put it on again for the people who missed it.' Mistress Christia could have been the only witness to the original display. She was always the first to arrive anywhere.

'Come on, Jherek. Everyone's to go to Wolverhampton. That's where we'll be shown the surprise.'

'Very well.' Jherek let her take his hand and lead him towards Wolverhampton, on the far side of the collection of cities.

And then suddenly all the flames went out and they were in complete darkness.

Silence fell.

'Delicious,' whispered Mistress Christia, squeezing his hand.

Jherek closed his eyes.

CHAPTER THREE

A VISITOR WHO IS LESS THAN ENTERTAINING

At last, after a longer pause than Jherek would have thought absolutely necessary, the voice of the Duke of Queens came to them through the darkness.

'Dear friends, you have doubtless already guessed that this party has a theme. That theme, needless to say, is "Disaster".'

A cool, soft voice said to Jherek: 'It's interesting to compare this expression of the theme with that of the Earl of Carbolic who gave it to us two years ago.'

Jherek smiled as he recognised Lord Jagged's voice. 'Wait for the lights to go up,' he said.

And then the lights did come on. They focused upon an odd, asymmetrical sort of mound which had been set on a dais of transparent steel. The mound seemed covered with a greenish-yellow mould. The mould pulsed. It made small squeaking sounds. It was less than charming.

'Well,' whispered Lord Jagged, still in darkness, for only the mound itself was lit, 'it certainly appears to fit the theme: what disaster could have caused that, I wonder!'

Mistress Christia squeezed Jherek's hand tighter and giggled. 'One of the Duke's experiments gone wrong, I'd have thought. Or perhaps the Duke himself?'

'Ah,' said Lord Jagged. 'How intelligent you are, Mistress Christia. As well as desirable, of course.'

The Duke of Queens, still unseen, continued with his introduction:

'This, my friends, is a spaceship. It landed near here a day or two ago.'

Jherek was disappointed and he could tell from their silence that the rest of the guests were just as disappointed. It was not unusual for spaceships to come to the planet, although none had called here in the last few years, as he remembered.

'It has come the furthest of any spaceship ever to visit our old

Earth,' said the voice of the Duke of Queens. 'It's travelled simply millions of light years to get here! Sensational in itself!'

This was still not good enough, thought Jherek, to make such a fuss about.

'Travelling at much the fastest speed of any spaceship to visit us before! Stupendous speed!' continued the Duke.

Jherek shrugged.

'Astounding,' came Lord Jagged's dry voice from beside him. 'A scientific lecture. The Duke of Queens is taking a leaf out of Li Pao's book. I suppose it makes a change. But somewhat out of character for our Duke, I'd have thought.'

'Perhaps even he has tired of sensationalism for its own sake,' said Jherek. 'But a rather dramatic reaction, surely?'

'Ah, these problems of taste. They'll remain a subject of debate until every one of us decides to end his existence, I fear.' Lord Jagged sighed.

'But you are thinking that this is not of sufficient moment to make a great fuss about,' said the Duke of Queens, as if in answer to Jherek and Lord Jagged. 'And, of course, you are right. The occupant of this particular spacecraft by coincidence happened to bring a certain amplification to the theme of my party tonight. I felt he would amuse you all. So here he is. His name, as far as I can pronounce it at all, is Yusharisp. He will address you through his own translation system (which is not quite of the quality to which we are used) and I'm sure you will find him as delightful as did I when I first spoke with him a little while ago. My dear friends, I give you the space-traveller Yusharisp.'

The light dimmed and then refocused on a creature standing on the other side of the transparent steel dais. The creature was about four feet tall, stood upon four bandy legs, had a round body, no head and no arms. Near the top of the body was a row of circular eyes, dotted at regular intervals about the entire circumference. There was a small triangular opening below these, which Jherek took to be the mouth. The creature was predominantly dark, muddy brown, with little flecks of green here and there. The eyes were bright, china blue. All in all, the space-traveller had a rather sour look to him.

'Greetings, people of this planet,' began Yusharisp. 'I come from the civilisation of Pweeli'—here the translator he was using screeched for a few seconds and Yusharisp had to cough to readjust it—'many galaxies distant. It is my self-appointed mission to travel the universe bringing with me my message. I believe it to be my duty to tell all intelligent life-forms what I know. I srrti oowo . . .' again a pause and a cough while Yusharisp adjusted his translator, which seemed to be a mechanical rather than an organic device of some kind, probably implanted in his equivalent of a throat by crude surgery. Jherek was interested in the device for its own sake, for he had heard of such things existing in the 19th century, or possibly a little later. 'I apologise,' Yusharisp continued, 'for the inefficiency of my equipment. It has been put to much use over the past two or three thousand years as I have travelled the universe bearing my tidings. After I leave here, I will continue my work until, at last, I perish. It will be several thousand years more before everyone I can possibly warn has been warned.' There was a sudden roaring and Jherek thought at first that it must be the lions, for he could not imagine a sound like it issuing from the tiny mouth cavity. But it was plain, from the alien's embarrassed gestures and coughs, that the translator was again malfunctioning. Jherek began to feel impatient.

'Well, I suppose it *is* an experience,' said Lord Jagged. 'Though I'm not sure that it was entirely tactful of the Duke of Queens to make it impossible for us to leave should we so desire. After all, not everyone enjoys being bored.'

'Oh, you are not kind, Lord Jagged,' said the equally invisible Mistress Christia. 'I feel a certain sympathy for the little creature.'

'Dry sgog,' said the alien. 'I am sorry. Dry sgog.' He cleared his throat again. 'I had best be as brief as possible.'

The guests were beginning to talk quite loudly among themselves now.

'In short,' said the alien, trying to make himself heard above a rising babble, 'my people have reached the inescapable conclusion that we are living at what you might call the End of Time. The universe is about to undergo a reformation of such massive proportions that not an atom of it will remain the same. All life will, effectively, die. All suns and planets will be destroyed as the universe ends one cycle and begins another. We are doomed, fellow intelligences. We are doomed.'

Jherek yawned. He wished the alien would get to the point. He began to stroke Mistress Christia's breasts.

The babble died. It was obvious that everyone was now waiting for the alien to finish.

'I see you are shocked, skree, skree, skree,' said the alien. 'Perhaps I could have (roar) put the news more tactfully, but I, skree, skree, have so little time. There is nothing we can do, of course, to avert our fate. We can only prepare ourselves, philosophically, skree, skree, for (roar) death.'

Mistress Christia giggled. She and Jherek sank to the ground and Jherek tried to remember how the lower garment of his set was removed. Mistress Christia's had already drifted open to receive him.

'Buttons,' said Jherek, who had not forgotten even this small detail.

'Isn't that amazing!' said the voice of the Duke of Queens. The voice was strained; it was disappointed; it was eager to infect them with the interest which he himself felt but which, it appeared, had failed to communicate itself to his guests. 'The end of the universe! Delightful!'

'I suppose so,' said Lord Jagged, feeling for Jherek's heaving back and patting it good-bye. 'But it is not a very *new* idea, is it?'

'We are all going to *die!*' The Duke of Queens laughed rather mechanically. 'Oh, it's delicious!'

'Good-bye, Jherek. Farewell, beautiful Mistress Christia.' Lord Jagged went away. It was plain that he was disappointed in the Duke of Queens; offended, even.

'Good-bye, Lord Jagged,' said Mistress Christia and Jherek together. Really, there hadn't been such a dull party in a thousand years. They separated and sat side by side on the lawn. By the sound of it, many others were drifting away, stumbling against people in the dark and apologising. It was, indeed, a disaster.

Jherek, now trying to be generous to the Duke of Queens, wondered if the thing had been deliberately engineered. Well, it was a relatively *fresh* experience—a party which failed.

The cities of Africa burst into flame once again and Jherek could see the dais and the Duke of Queens standing talking to the alien on the dais.

Lady Charlotina went past, not noticing Jherek and Mistress Christia who were still sitting on the ground.

'Duke,' called Lady Charlotina, 'is your friend part of your menagerie?'

The Duke of Queens turned, his fine, bearded face full of dejection. It was obvious that he had not planned the failure at all.

'He must be tired, poor thing,' said Mistress Christia.

'It was almost bound to happen. Sensation piled on sensation but rooted in nothing, no proper artistic conception,' said Jherek maliciously. 'It is what I've always said.'

'Oh, Jherek. Don't be unkind.'

'Well . . .' Jherek did feel ashamed of himself. He had been on the point of revelling in the Duke's appalling mistake. 'Very well, Mistress Christia. You and I shall go and comfort him. Congratulate him, if you like, though I fear he won't believe in my sincerity.' They got up.

The Duke of Queens was taken aback by Lady Charlotina's question. He said vaguely: 'Menagerie? Why, no . . .'

'Then might I have him?'

'Yes, yes, of course.'

'Thank you.' Lady Charlotina gestured to the alien. 'Will you come with me, please.'

The alien turned several of his eyes upon her. 'But I must leave. My message. You are kind to, skree, skree, invite, skree, me. Howev (roar) er, I shall have to, skree, decline.' He began to move towards his ship.

Regretfully Lady Charlotina gestured with one hand and froze the alien while with the other hand she disseminated his spaceship.

'Disgusting!'

Jherek heard the voice behind him and turned, delightedly, to identify it. The person had spoken in the language of the 19th century. A woman stood there. She wore a tight-fitting grey jacket and a voluminous grey skirt which covered all but the toes of her black boots. Beneath the jacket could just be seen a white blouse with a small amount of lacework on the bodice. She had a straw, wide-brimmed hat upon her heavily coiled chestnut hair and an expression of outrage on her pretty, heart-shaped face. A time-traveller, without doubt. Jherek grinned with pleasure.

'Oh!' he exclaimed. 'An ancient!'

She ignored him, calling out to Lady Charlotina (who, of course, did not understand 19th century speech at all): *'Let the poor creature go! Though he is neither human nor Christian, he is still one of God's creatures and has a right to his liberty!'*

Jherek was speechless with delight as he watched the time-traveller stride forward, the heavy skirts swinging. Mistress Christia raised her eyebrows. 'What is she saying, Jherek?'

'She must be new,' he said. 'She has yet to take a translation pill.

She seems to want the little alien for herself. I don't understand every word, of course.' He shook his head in admiration as the time-traveller laid a small hand upon Lady Charlotina's shoulder. Lady Charlotina turned in surprise.

Jherek and Mistress Christia approached the pair. The Duke of Queens peered down from the dais looking first at them and then at the frozen space creature without any understanding at all.

'*What you have done you can undo, degenerate soul,*' said the time-traveller to the bewildered Lady Charlotina.

'She's speaking 19th century—one of many dialects,' explained Jherek, proud of his knowledge.

Lady Charlotina inspected the grey-clad woman. 'Does she want to make love to me? I suppose I will, if . . .'

Jherek shook his head. 'No. I think she wants your alien. Or, perhaps, she doesn't want you to have it. I'll speak to her. Just a moment.' He turned and smiled at the ancient.

'*Good evening, fräulein. I parle the yazhak. Năy m̃-sai pă,*' said Jherek.

She did not appear to be reassured. But now she stared at him in equal astonishment.

'*The fräulein this,*' said Jherek, indicating Lady Charlotina, who listened with mild interest, '*is pense que t'a make love to elle.*' He was about to continue and point out that he knew that this was not the case when the time-traveller transferred her attention to him altogether and delivered a heavy smack on his cheek. This baffled him. He had no knowledge of the custom or, indeed, how to respond to it.

'I think,' he said to Lady Charlotina regretfully, 'that we ought to give her a pill before we go any further.'

'*Disgusting!*' said the time-traveller again. '*I shall seek someone in authority. This must be stopped. I'm beginning to believe I've had the misfortune to find myself in a colony of lunatics!*'

They all watched her stalk away.

'Isn't she fine,' said Jherek. 'I wonder if anyone's claimed her. It almost makes me want to start my own menagerie.'

The Duke of Queens lowered himself from the dais and settled beside them. He was dressed in a force-form chastity belt, feather cloak and had a conical hat of shrunken human heads. 'I must apologise,' he began.

'The whole thing was superb,' said Jherek, all malice forgotten in his delight at meeting the time-traveller. 'How did you think of it?'

'Well,' said the Duke of Queens fingering his beard. 'Ah . . .'

'A wonderful joke, juiciest of Dukes,' said Mistress Christia. 'We shall be talking about it for days!'

'Oh?' The Duke of Queens brightened.

'And you have shown your enormous kindness once again,' said Lady Charlotina, pressing her sky blue lips and nose to his cheek, 'in giving me the morbid space-traveller for my menagerie. I haven't got a round one.'

'Of course, of course,' said the Duke of Queens, his normal ebullience returning, though Jherek thought that the Duke rather regretted making the gift.

The Lady Charlotina made an adjustment to one of her rings and the stiff body of the little alien floated from the dais and hovered over her head, bobbing slightly in the manner of a captive balloon.

Jherek said: 'The time-traveller. Is she yours, My Lord Duke?'

'The grey one who slapped you? No. I've never seen her before. Perhaps a maverick?'

'Perhaps so.' Jherek took off his opera hat and made a sweeping bow to the company. 'If you will forgive me, then, I'll see if I can find her. She will add a touch to my present collection which will bring it close to perfection. Farewell.'

'Good-bye, Jherek,' said the Duke, almost gratefully. Sympathetically Lady Charlotina and Mistress Christia took each of his arms and led him away while Jherek bowed once more and then struck off in pursuit of his quarry.

CHAPTER FOUR

CARNELIAN CONCEIVES A NEW AFFECTATION

AFTER an hour of searching, Jherek realised that the grey time-traveller was no longer at the party. Because most of the guests had left, it had not been a difficult search. Disconsolate, he returned to his locomotive and swung aboard, throwing himself upon the long seat of plush and ermine, but hesitating before he pulled the whistle and set the aircar in motion, for he wanted something to happen to him—a compensation for his disappointment.

Either, he thought, the time-traveller had been returned to the menagerie of whomever it was that owned her, or else she had gone somewhere of her own volition. He hoped that she did not have a time-travelling machine capable of carrying her back to her own age. If she had, then it was likely she was gone forever. He seemed to remember that there was some evidence to suggest that the people of the late 19th century had possessed a crude form of time-travel.

'Ah, well,' he sighed to himself, 'if she has gone, she has gone.'

His mother, the Iron Orchid, had left with the Lady Voiceless and Ulianov of the Palms, doubtless to revive memories of times before he had been born. Being naturally gregarious, he felt deserted. There was hardly anyone left whom he knew well or would care to take back with him to his ranch. He wanted the time-traveller. His heart was set on her. She was charming. He fingered his cheek and smiled.

Peering through one of the observation windows, he saw Mongrove and Werther de Goethe approaching and he stood up to hail them. But both pointedly ignored him and so increased his sense of desolation where normally he would have been amused by the perfection with which they played their roles. He slumped, once more, into his cushions, now thoroughly reluctant to return home but with no idea of any alternative. Mistress Christia, always a willing companion, had gone off with the Duke of Queens and My Lady Charlotina. Even Li Pao was nowhere to be seen. He yawned and closed his eyes.

'Sleeping, my dear?'

It was Lord Jagged. He stood peering up over the footplate. 'Is this the machine you were telling me about. The——?'

'The locomotive. Oh, Lord Jagged, I am so pleased to see you. I thought you left hours ago.'

'I was diverted.' The pale head emerged a fraction further from the yellow collar. 'And then deserted.' Lord Jagged smiled his familiar, wistful smile. 'May I join you?'

'Of course.'

Lord Jagged floated up, a cloud of lemon-coloured down, and sat beside Jherek.

'So the Duke's display was not a deliberate disaster?' said Lord Jagged. 'But we all pretended that it was.'

Jherek Carnelian drew off his opera hat and flung it from the locomotive. It became a puff of orange smoke which dissipated in the air. He loosened the cord of his cloak. 'Yes,' he said, 'even I managed to compliment him. He was so miserable. But what could have possessed him to think that anyone would be interested in an ordinary little alien? And a mad, prophesying one, at that.'

'You don't think he told the truth, then? The alien?'

'Oh, yes. I'm sure he spoke the truth. Why shouldn't he? But what is particularly interesting about the *truth*? Very little, when it comes down to it, as we all know. Look at Li Pao. He is forever telling the truth, too. And what is a truth, anyway? There are so many different kinds.'

'And his message did not disturb you?'

'His message? No. The lifetime of the universe is finite. That was his message.'

'And we are near the end of that lifetime. He said that.' Lord Jagged made a motion with his hand and disrobed himself, stretching his thin, pale body upon the couch.

'Why are you making so much of this, white Lord Jagged?'

Lord Jagged laughed. 'I am not. I am not. Just conversation. And a touch or two of curiosity. Your mind is so much fresher than mine —than almost anyone's in the world. That is why I ask questions. If it bores you I'll stop.'

'No. The poor little space-traveller was a bore, wasn't he? Wasn't he, Lord Jagged. Or did you find something interesting about him?'

'Not really. People used to fear death once, you know, and I suppose whatever-his-name-was still fears it. I believe that people used to wish to communicate their fear. To spread it somehow comforted them. I suppose that is his impulse. Well, he shall find plenty to comfort him in My Lady Charlotina's menagerie.'

'Speaking of menageries, did you see a girl time-traveller dressed in rather heavy grey garments, wearing a straw-coloured hat with a wide brim, at the party?'

'I believe I did.'

'Did you notice where she went? Did you see her leave?'

'I think Mongrove took a fancy to her and sent her in his aircar to his menagerie before he left with Werther de Goethe.'

'Mongrove! How unfortunate.'

'You wanted her yourself?'

'Yes.'

'But you've no menagerie.'

'I have a 19th century collection. She would have suited it perfectly.'

'She's 19th century, then?'

'Yes.'

'Perhaps Mongrove will give her to you.'

'Mongrove had best not know I want her at all. He would disseminate her or send her back to her own time or give her away rather than think he was contributing to my pleasure. You must know that, Lord Jagged.'

'You couldn't trade something for her. What about the item Mongrove wanted from you so much? The elderly writer—from the same period, wasn't he?'

'Yes, before I became interested in it. I remember, Ambrose Bierce.'

'The same!'

'He went up with the others. In the fire. I couldn't be bothered to reconstitute him and now, of course, it's too late.'

'You were never prudent, tender Jherek.'

Jherek's brows knitted. 'I *must* have her, Lord Jagged, I think, in fact, that I shall fall in love with her. Yes! in *love*.'

'Oho!' Lord Jagged threw back his head, arching his exquisite neck. 'Love! Love! How splendid, Jherek.'

'I will plunge into it. I will encourage the passion until I am as involved in it as Mongrove is involved in his misery.'

'An excellent affectation. It will power your mind. It will make you so ingenious. You will succeed. You will get her away from Mongrove, though it will turn the world upside down! You will entertain us all. You will thrill us. You will hold our attention for months! For years! We shall speculate upon your success or your failure. We shall wonder how far you have really involved yourself in this game. We shall watch to see how your grey time-traveller responds. Will she return your love? Will she spurn it? Will she decide to love Mongrove, the more to complicate your schemes?' Lord Jagged reached over and kissed Jherek heartily upon the lips. 'Yes! It must be played out in every small detail. Your friends will help. They will give you tips. They'll consult the literatures of the ages to glean the best of the love stories and you will act them out. Gorgon and Queen Elizabeth. Romeo and Julius Caesar. Windermere and Lady Oscar. Hitler and Mussolini. Fred and Louella. Ojiba and Obija. Sero and Fidsekalak. The list goes on—and on! And on, dear Jherek!'

Fired by his friend's enthusiasm Jherek stood up and yelled with laughter.

'I shall be a *lover!*'

'A lover!'

'Nothing shall thwart me!'

'Nothing!'

'I shall win my love and live with her in ardent happiness until the very universe grows old and cold.'

'Or whatever our space-travelling friend said would happen. Now that factor should give it an edge.' Lord Jagged fingered his linen-coloured nose. 'Oh, you'll be doomed, desired, deceived, debunked and delivered!' (Lord Jagged seemed to be fond, tonight, of his d's.) 'Demonic, demonstrative, determined, destructive.' He was dangerously close to overdoing it. 'You'll be destiny's fool, my dear! Your story shall ring down the ages (whatever's left, at any rate). Jherek Carnelian—the most laudable, the most laborious, the most literal, the very *last* of lovers!' And with a yell he flung his arms around his friend while Jherek Carnelian seized the whistle string and tugged wildly making the locomotive shriek and moan and thrust itself throbbing into the warm, black night.

'Love!' shouted Jherek.

'Love,' whispered Lord Jagged, kissing him once more.

'Oh, Jagged!' Jherek gave himself up to his lascivious lord's embrace.

'She must have a name,' said Jagged, rolling over in the eight-poster bed and taking a sip of beer from the bronze barrel he held between the forefinger and thumb of his left hand. 'We must find it out.' He got up and crossed the corrugated iron floor to brush aside the sheets from the window and peer through. 'Is that a sunset or a sunrise? It looks like a sunset.'

'I'm sorry.' Jherek opened his eyes and turned one of his rings a fraction of a degree to the right.

'Much better,' said Lord Jagged of Canaria, admiring the golden dawn. 'And what are the birds?' He pointed through the window at the black silhouettes circling high above in the sky.

'Parrots,' said Jherek. 'They're supposed to eat the branded buffalo.'

'Supposed to?'

'They won't. And they should be perfect reproductions. I made a mistake somewhere. I really ought to put them back in my gene-bank and start again.'

'What if we paid Mongrove a visit this morning?' Lord Jherek suggested, returning to his original subject.

'He wouldn't receive me.'

'He would receive *me*, however. And you will be my companion. I will feign an interest in his menagerie and that way you shall be able to meet again the object of your desire.'

'I'm not sure it's such a good idea now, darling Jagged,' said Jherek. 'I was carried away last night.'

'Indeed, my love, you were. And why not? How often does it happen? No, Jherek Carnelian, you shall not falter. It will delight so many.'

Jherek laughed. 'Lord Jagged, I think there is some other motive involved here—a motive of your own. Would you not rather take my place?'

'I? I have no interest at all in the period.'

'Aren't you interested in falling in love?'

'I am interested in *your* falling in love. You should. It will complete you, Jherek. You were *born*, do you see? The rest of us came into the world as adults (apart from poor Werther, but that was a somewhat different story) or created ourselves or were created by our friends. But you, Jherek, were born—a baby. And so you must also fall in love. Oh, yes. There is no question of it. In any other one of us it would be silly.'

'I think you have already pointed out that it would be ludicrous in me, too,' said Jherek mildly.

'Love was always *ludicrous,* Jherek. That's another thing again.'

'Very well,' smiled Jherek. 'To please you, my lean lord, I will do my best.'

'To please us all. Including yourself, Jherek. Especially yourself, Jherek.'

'I must admit that I might consider . . .'

Lord Jagged began, suddenly, to sing.

The notes trilled and warbled from his throat. A most delightful rush of song and such a complicated melody that Jherek could hardly follow it.

Jerek glanced thoughtfully and with some irony at his friend.

It had seemed for a moment that Lord Jagged had deliberately cut Jherek short.

But why?

He had only been about to point out that the Lord of Canaria had all the qualities of affection, wit and imagination that might be desired in a lover and that Jherek would willingly fall in love with him rather than some time-traveller whom he did not know at all.

And, Jherek suspected, Lord Jagged had known that he was about to say this. Would the declaration have been in doubtful taste, perhaps? The point about falling in love with the grey time-traveller was that she would find nothing strange in it. In her age *everyone* had fallen in love (or, at very least, had been able to deceive themselves that they had, which was much the same thing). Yes, Lord Jagged had acted with great generosity and stopped him from embarrassing himself. It would have been vulgar to have declared his love for Lord Jagged but it was witty to fall in love with the grey time-traveller.

Not that there was anything wrong with intentional vulgarity. Or even unintentional vulgarity, thought Jherek, in the case, for instance, of the Duke of Queens.

He recalled the party with horror. 'The poor Duke of Queens!'

'His party was absolutely perfect. Not a thing went right.' Lord Jagged left the window and wandered over the bumpy floor. 'May I use this for a suit?' He gestured towards a stuffed mammoth which filled one corner of the room.

'Of course,' said Jherek. 'I was never quite sure if it was in period, anyway. How clever of you to pick that.' He watched with interest as Lord Jagged broke the mammoth down into its component atoms and then, from the hovering cloud of particles, concocted for himself a loose, lilac-coloured robe with the kind of high, stiff collar he often favoured, and huge puffed sleeves from which peeped the tips of his fingers, and silver slippers with long, pointed toes, and a circlet to contain his long platinum hair; a circlet in the form of a rippling, living 54th century Uranian lizard.

'How haughty you look!' said Jherek. 'A prince of fifty planets!'

Lord Jagged bowed in acknowledgement of the compliment. 'We are the sum of all previous ages, are we not? And as a result there is nothing that marks this age of ours, save that one thing. We are the sum.'

'I had never thought of it.' Jherek swung his long legs from the bed and stood up.

'Nor I, until this moment. But it is true. I can think of nothing else typical. Our technologies, our tricks, our conceits—they all imitate the past. We benefit from everything our ancestors worked to achieve. But we invent nothing of our own—we merely ring a few changes on what already exists.'

'There is nothing left to invent, my lilac lord. The long history of mankind, if it has a purpose at all, has found complete fulfilment in us. We can indulge any fancy. We can choose to be whatever we wish and do whatever we wish. What else is there? We are happy. Even Mongrove is happy in his misery—it is his choice. No one would try to alter it. I am rather at a loss, therefore, to follow where your argument is leading.' Jherek sipped from his own beer barrel.

'There was no argument, my jaunty Jherek. It was an observation I made. That was all.'

'And accurate.' Jherek was at a loss to add anything more.

'Accurate.'

Lord Jagged stood back to admire Jherek, still unclothed for the day.

'And what will you wear?'

'I have been considering that very question.' Jherek put a finger to his chin. 'It must be in keeping with all this—especially since I am to pay court to a lady of the 19th century. But it cannot be the same as yesterday.'

'No,' agreed Lord Jagged.

And then Jherek had it. He was delighted at his own brilliance.

'I know! I shall wear exactly the same costume as she wore last night! It will be a compliment she cannot fail to notice.'

'Jherek,' crooned Lord Jagged, hugging him, 'you are the best of us!'

CHAPTER FIVE

A MENAGERIE OF TIME AND SPACE

'The very best of us,' yawned Lord Jagged of Canaria, lying back upon the couch of plush and ermine as Jherek, clad in his new costume, pulled the whistle of the locomotive which took off from the corral and left the West behind, heading for gloomy Mongrove's domain.

The locomotive steered a course for the tropics, passing through a dozen different skies. Some of the skies were still being completed, while others were being dismantled as their creators wearied of them.

They puffed over the old cities which nobody used any more, but which were not destroyed because the sources of many forms of energy were still stored there—the energy in particular, which powered the rings everyone wore. Once whole star systems had been converted to store the energy banks of Earth, during the manic Engineering Millennium, when everyone, it appeared, had devoted themselves to that single purpose.

They travelled through several daytimes and a few night-times on their way to Mongrove's. The giant, save for his brief Hellmaking fad, had always lived in the same place, where a subcontinent called Indi had once been. It was well over an hour before they sighted the grey clouds which perpetually hung over Mongrove's domain, pouring down either snow or sleet or hail or rain, depending on the giant's mood. The sun never shone through those clouds. Mongrove hated sunshine.

Lord Jagged pretended to shiver, though his garments had naturally adjusted to the change in temperature. 'There are Mongrove's miserable cliffs. I can see them now.' He pointed through the observation window.

Jherek looked and saw them. Mile high crags met the grey clouds. They were black, gleaming and melancholy crags, without symmetry, without a single patch of relieving colour, for even the rain which fell on them seemed to turn black as it struck them and ran in weeping black rivers down their rocky flanks. And Jherek shivered, too. It had been many years since he had visited Mongrove and he had forgotten with what uncompromising misery the giant had designed his home.

At a murmured command from Jherek, the locomotive rolled up the sky to get above the clouds. The rain and the cold would not affect the aircar, but Jherek found the mere sight too glum for his taste. But soon they had passed over the cliffs and Jherek could tell from the way in which the cloud bank seemed to dip in the middle that they were over Mongrove's valley. Now they would have to pass through the clouds. There was no choice.

The locomotive began to descend, passing through layer after grey layer of the thick, swirling mist until it emerged, finally, over Mongrove's valley. Jherek and Lord Jagged looked down upon a blighted landscape of festering marsh and leafless, stunted trees, of bleak boulders, of withered shrubs and dank moss. In the very centre of all this desolation squatted the vast, cheerless complex of buildings and enclosures which was surrounded by a great, glabrous wall and dominated by Mongrove's dark, obsidian castle. From the castle's ragged towers shone a few dim, yellowish lights.

Almost immediately a force dome appeared over the castle and its environs. It turned the falling rain to steam. Then Mongrove's voice, amplified fiftyfold, boomed from the now partially hidden castle:

'What enemy approaches to plague and threaten despondent Mongrove?'

Although Mongrove's detectors would already have identified them, Jagged answered with good humour.

'It is I, dear Mongrove. Your good friend Lord Jagged of Canaria.'

'And another.'

'Yes, another. Jherek Carnelian is well known to you, surely?'

'Well known and well hated. He is not welcome here, Lord Jagged.'

'And I? Am I not welcome?'

'None are welcome at Castle Mongrove, but you may enter, if you wish.'

'And my friend Jherek?'

'If you insist upon bringing him with you—and if I have his word, Lord Jagged, that he is not here to play one of his cruel jests upon me.'

'You have my word, Mongrove,' said Jherek.

'Then,' said Mongrove reluctantly, 'enter.'

The force dome vanished; the rain fell unhindered upon the basalt and the obsidian. For the sake of politeness, Jherek did not take his locomotive over the wall. Instead he brought the aircar to the swampy ground and waited until the massive iron gates groaned open just wide enough to admit the locomotive, which shuffled merrily through, giving out multicoloured smoke from its funnel and its bogies—a most incongruous sight and one which was bound to displease Mongrove. Yet Jherek could not resist it. Mongrove desired so much to be baited, he felt, and he desired so much to bait him that he let few opportunities go. Lord Jagged placed a hand on Jherek's shoulder.

'It would improve matters and make our task the easier if we were to forgo the smoke, jolly Jherek.'

'Very well!' Jherek laughed and ordered the smoke to stop. 'Perhaps I should have designed a more funereal carriage altogether. For the occasion. One of those black ships of the Four Year Empire would do. Oh, death meant so much to them in those days. Are we missing something, I wonder?'

'I have wondered that. Still, we have all of us died so many times and been recreated so many times that the thrill is gone. For them —especially the heavy folk of the Four Year Empire—it was an experience they could have only three or four times at most before their systems gave out. Strange.'

They were nearing the main entrance of the castle itself, passing through narrow streets full of lowering, dark walls and iron fences behind which dim shapes could be seen moving occasionally. The large part of all this was Mongrove's menagerie.

'He has added a great deal to it since I was last here,' said Jherek. 'I hadn't realised.'

'You had best follow my lead,' said Lord Jagged. 'I will gauge Mongrove's mood and ask, casually, if we can see the menagerie. Perhaps after lunch, if he offers us lunch.'

'I remember the last lunch I had here,' Jherek said with a shudder. 'Raw Turyian dungwhale prepared in the style of the Zhadash primitives who hunted it, I gather, on Ganesha in the 89th century.'

'You do remember it well.'

'I could never forget it. I have never questioned Mongrove's *artistry*, Lord Jagged. Like me, he is a stickler for detail.'

'And that is why this rivalry exists between you, I shouldn't wonder. You are of similar temperaments, really.'

Jherek laughed. 'Perhaps. Though I think I prefer the way in which I *express* mine!'

They went under a portcullis and entered a cobbled courtyard. The locomotive stopped.

Rain fell on the cobbles. Somewhere a sad bell tolled and tolled and tolled.

And there was Mongrove. He was dressed in dark green robes, his great chin sunk upon his huge chest, his brooding eyes regarding them from a head which seemed itself carved from rock. His monstrous, ten-foot frame did not move as they dismounted from the aircar and, from politeness, allowed themselves to be soaked by the chill rain.

'Good morning, Mongrove.' Lord Jagged of Canaria made one of his famous sweeping bows and then tip-toed forward to reach up and grasp the giant's bulky hands which were folded on his stomach.

'Jagged,' said Mongrove. 'I am feeling suspicious. Why are you and that wretch Jherek Carnelian here? What plot's hatching? What devious brew are you boiling? What new ruse are you rascals ripening to make a rift in my peace of mind.'

'Oh, come, Mongrove—peace of mind! Isn't that the last thing you desire?' Jherek could not resist the jibe. He stood before his old rival in his new grey gown with his straw boater upon his chestnut curls and his hands on his hips and he grinned up at the giant. 'It is despair you seek—exquisite despair. It is agony of soul such as the ancients knew. You wish to discover the secret of what they called "the human condition" and recreate it in all its terror and its pain. And yet you have never quite discovered that secret, have you, Mongrove? Is that why you keep this vast menagerie with creatures culled from all the ages, all the places of the universe? Do you hope that, in their misery, they will show you the way from despair to utter despair, from melancholy to the deepest melancholy, from gloom to unspeakable gloom?'

'Be silent!' groaned Mongrove. 'You *did* come here to plague me. You cannot stay! You cannot stay!' He covered his monstrous ears with his monstrous hands and closed his great, sad eyes.

'I apologise for Jherek, Mongrove,' said Lord Jagged softly. 'He only hopes to please you.'

Mongrove's reply was in the form of a vast, shuddering moan. He began to turn, to go back into his castle.

'Please, Mongrove,' said Jherek. 'I do apologise. I really do. I wish there was some release for you from this terror, this gloom, this unbearable depression.'

Mongrove turned back again, brightening just a trifle. 'You understand?"

'Of course. Though I have felt only a fraction of what you must feel—I understand.' Jherek placed his hand on his bosom. 'The aching sorrow of it all.'

'Yes,' whispered Mongrove. A tear fell from his huge right eye. 'That is very true, Jherek.' A tear fell from his left eye. 'Nobody understands, as a rule. I am a joke. A laughing-stock. They know that in this great frame is a tiny, frightened, pathetic creature incapable of any generosity, without creative talent, with a capacity only to weep, to mourn, to sigh and to watch the tragedy that is human life play itself to its awful conclusion.'

'Yes,' said Jherek. 'Yes, Mongrove.'

Lord Jagged, who now stood behind Mongrove, sheltering in the doorway of the castle and leaning against the obsidian wall, gave Jherek a look of pure admiration and added to this look one of absolute approval. He nodded his pale head. He smiled. He winked his encouragement, the white lid falling over his almost colourless eye.

Jherek did admire Mongrove for the pains he took to make his role complete. When he, Jherek, became a lover, he would pursue his role with the same dedication.

'You see,' said Lord Jagged. 'You see, Mongrove. Jherek understands and sympathises better than anyone. In the past he has played the odd practical joke upon you, it is true, but that was because he was trying to cheer you up. Before he realised that nothing can hope to ease the misery in your bleak soul and so on.'

'Yes,' said Mongrove. 'I do see, Lord Jagged.' He threw a huge arm around Jherek's shoulders and almost flung Jherek to the cobbled ground, muddying his skirts. Jherek feared for his set. It was already getting wet and yet politeness forbade him to use any form of force protection. He felt his straw hat begin to sag a little. He looked down at his blouse and saw that the lace was looking a bit straggly.

'Come,' Mongrove went on. 'You shall lunch with me. My honoured guests. I never realised before, Jherek, how sensitive you were. And you tried to hide your sensitivity with rough humour, with coarse badinage and crude japes.'

Jherek thought many of his jokes had been rather subtle, but it was not politic to say so at the moment. He nodded, instead, and smiled.

Mongrove led them at last into the castle. For all the winds whistling through the passages and howling along stairwells; for all that the only light was from guttering brands and that the walls ran with damp or were festooned with mildew; for all the rats glimpsed from time to time; for all the bloodless faces of Mongrove's living-dead retainers, the thick cobwebs, the chilly odours, the peculiar little sounds, Jherek was pleased to be inside and walked quite merrily with Mongrove as they made their way up several flights of unclad stone stairs, through a profusion of twisting corridors until at last they arrived in Mongrove's banqueting hall.

'And where is Werther,' asked Lord Jagged, 'de Goethe, I mean? I was sure he left with you last night. At the Duke of Queens?'

'The Duke of Queens.' Mongrove's massive brow frowned. 'Aye. Aye. The Duke of Queens. Yes, Werther was here for a while. But he left. Some new nightmare or other he promised to show me when he'd completed it.'

'Nightmare?'

'A play. Something. I'm not sure. He said I would like it.'

'Excellent.'

'Ah,' sighed Mongrove. 'That space-traveller. How I would love to converse longer with him. Did you hear him? Doom, he said. We are *doomed!*'

'Doom, doom,' echoed Lord Jagged, signing for Jherek to join in.

'Doom,' said Jherek a little uncertainly. 'Doom, doom.'

'Yes, dark damnation. Dejection. Doom. Doom. Doom.' Mongrove stared into the middle distance.

Jherek thought that Mongrove seemed to have picked up Lord Jagged's predilection for words beginning with d.

'You covet, then, the alien?' he said.

'Covet him?'

'You want him in your menagerie?' explained Lord Jagged. 'That's the question.'

'Of course I would like him here. He is very *morbid,* isn't he? He would make an excellent companion.'

'Oh, he would!' said Lord Jagged, staring significantly at Jherek as the three men seated themselves at Mongrove's chipped and stained dining table. But Jherek couldn't quite work out why Jagged stared at him significantly. 'He would! What a shame he is in My Lady's Charlotina's collection.'

'Is that where he is? I wondered.'

'Lady Charlotina wouldn't *give* you the little alien, I suppose,' said Lord Jagged. 'Since his companionship would mean so much to you.'

'Lady Charlotina hates me,' said Mongrove simply.

'Surely not!'

'Oh, yes she does. She would give me nothing. She is jealous of my collection, I suppose.' Mongrove went on, with gloomy pride: 'My collection is large. Possibly the largest there is.'

'I have heard that it is magnificent,' Jherek told him.

'Thank you, Jherek,' said the giant gratefully.

Mongrove's attitude had changed completely. Evidently all he asked for was that his misery should be taken seriously. Then he could forget every past slight, every joke at his expense, that Jherek had ever made. In a few minutes they had changed, in Mongrove's eyes, from being bitter enemies to the closest of friends.

It was plain to Jherek that Lord Jagged understood Mongrove very well—as well as he knew Jherek, if not better. He was constantly astonished at the insight of the Lord of Canaria. Sometimes Lord Jagged could appear almost sinister!

'I would very much like to see your menagerie,' said Lord Jagged. 'Would that be possible, my miserable Mongrove?'

'Of course, of course,' said Mongrove. 'There is little to see, really. I expect it lacks the glamour of My Lady Charlotina's, the colour of the Duke of Queens', even the variety of your mother's, Jherek, the Iron Orchid's.'

'I am sure that is not the case,' said Jherek diplomatically.

'And would you like to see my menagerie also?' asked Mongrove.

'Very much,' said Jherek. 'Very much. I hear you have——'

'Those cracks,' said Lord Jagged suddenly and deliberately interrupting his friend, 'they are new, are they not, dear Mongrove?'

He gestured towards several large fissures in the far wall of the hall.

'Yes, they're comparatively recent,' Mongrove agreed. 'Do you like them?'

'They are *prime!*'

'Not excessive? You don't think they are excessive?' Mongrove asked anxiously.

'Not a bit. They are just right. The touch of a true artist.'

'I'm so glad, Lord Jagged, that two men of such understanding taste have visited me. You must forgive me if earlier I seemed surly.'

'Surly? No, no. Naturally cautious, yes. But not surly.'

'We must eat,' said Mongrove and Jherek's heart sank. 'Lunch— and then I'll show you round my menagerie.'

Mongrove clapped his hands and food appeared on the table.

'Splendid!' said Lord Jagged, surveying the discoloured meats and the watery vegetables, the withered salads and lumpy dressings. 'And what are these delicacies?'

'It is a banquet of the time of the Kalean Plague Century,' said Mongrove proudly. 'You've heard of the plague? It swept the Solar System in, I think, the 1000th century. It infected everyone and everything.'

'Wonderful,' said Lord Jagged with what seemed to be genuine enthusiasm. Jherek, struggling to restrain an expression of nausea, was amazed at his friend's self-control.

'And what,' said Lord Jagged, picking up a dish on which sat a piece of quivering, bloody flesh, 'would this be?'

'Well, it's my own reproduction, of course, but I think it's authentic.' Mongrove half-rose to peer at the dish, looming over the pair. 'Ah, yes—that's Snort—or is it Snout? It's confusing. I've studied all I could of the period. One of my favourites. If it's Snort, they had to change their entire religious attitude in order to justify eating it. If it's Snout, I'm not sure it would be wise for you to eat it. Although, if you've never died from food-poisoning, it's an interesting experience.'

'I never have,' said Lord Jagged. 'But on the other hand, it would take a while, I suppose, and I was rather keen to see your menagerie this afternoon.'

'Perhaps another time, then,' said Mongrove politely, though it seemed he was a trifle disappointed. 'Snout is one of my favourites. Or is it Snort? But I had better resist the temptation, too. Jherek?'

Jherek reached for the nearest dish. 'This looks tasty.'

'Well, *tasty* is not the word I'd choose.' Mongrove uttered a strange, humourless laugh. 'Very little Plague Century food was that. Indeed, taste is not the criterion I apply in planning my meals . . .'

'No, no,' nodded Jherek. 'I meant it looked—um . . .'

'Diseased?' suggested Lord Jagged, munching his new choice (very little different in appearance from the Snout or Snort he had rejected) with every apparent relish.

Jherek looked at Mongrove, who nodded his approval of Lord Jagged's description.

'Yes,' said Jherek in a small, strangled voice. 'Diseased.'

'It was. But it will do you no great harm. They had slightly different metabolisms, as you can imagine.' Mongrove pushed the dish towards Jherek. In it was some kind of greenish vegetable in a brown, murky sauce. 'Help yourself.'

Jherek ladled the smallest possible amount on to his plate.

'More,' said Mongrove, munching. 'Have more. There's plenty.'

'More,' whispered Jherek, and heaped another spoonful or two from the dish to his plate.

He had never had much of an appetite for crude food at the best of times, preferring more direct (and invisible) means of sustaining himself. And this was the most ghastly crude food he had ever seen in his entire life.

He began to wish that he had suggested they have the Turyian dungwhale, after all.

At last the ordeal ended and Mongrove got up, wiping his lips.

Jherek, who had been concentrating on controlling his spasms as he forced the food down his throat, noticed that while Lord Jagged had eaten with every sign of heartiness he had actually consumed very little. He must get Jagged to teach him that trick.

'And now,' said Mongrove, 'my menagerie awaits us.' He looked with despondent kindness upon Jherek, who had not yet risen. 'Are you unwell? Perhaps the food was more diseased than it should have been?'

'Perhaps,' said Jherek, pressing his palms on the wood of the table and pushing his body upright.

'Do you feel dizzy?' asked Mongrove, grasping Jherek's elbow to support him.

'A little.'

'Are there pains in the stomach? Have you a stomach?'

'I think I have. There *are* a few small pains.'

'Hmm.' Mongrove frowned. 'Maybe we should make the tour another day.'

'No, no,' said Jagged. 'Jherek will appreciate things all the more if he is feeling a little low. He enjoys feeling low. It brings him closer to a true understanding of the essential pain of human existence. Doesn't it, Jherek?'

Jherek moved his head up and down in assent. He could not quite bring himself to speak to Lord Jagged at that moment.

'Very good,' said Mongrove, propelling Jherek forward. 'Very good. I wish that we had settled our differences much earlier, gentle Jherek. I can see now how much I have misunderstood you.'

And Jherek, while Mongrove's attention was diverted, darted a look of pure hatred at his friend Lord Jagged.

He had recovered a little by the time they left the courtyard and plodded through the rain to the first menagerie building. Here Mongrove kept his collection of bacteria; his viruses, his cancers—all magnified by screens, some of which measured nearly an eighth of a mile across. Mongrove seemed to have an affinity with plagues.

'Some of these illnesses are more than a million years old,' he said proudly. 'Brought by time-travellers, mostly. Others come from all over the universe. We have missed a lot, you know, my friends, by not having diseases of our own.'

He paused before one of the larger screens. Here were examples of how the bacteria infected the creatures from which they had originally been taken.

A bearlike alien writhed in agony as his flesh bubbled and burst.

A reptilian space-traveller sat and watched with bleary eyes as his webbed hands and feet grew small tentacles which gradually wrapped themselves around the rest of his body and strangled him.

'I sometimes wonder if we, the most imaginative of creatures, lack a certain kind of imagination,' murmured Lord Jagged to Jherek as they paused to look at the poor reptile.

Elsewhere a floral intelligence was attacked by a fungus which gradually ate at its beautiful blossoms and turned its stems to dry twigs.

There were hundreds of them. They were all so interesting that Jherek began to forget his own qualms and left Jagged behind as he strode beside Mongrove, asking questions and, often, giving close attention to the answers.

Lord Jagged was inclined to linger, examining this specimen, exclaiming about that one, and was late in following them when they left the Bacteria House and entered the Fluctuant House.

43

Here was a wide variety of creatures which could change shape or colour at will. Each creature was allowed a large space of its own in which its environment had been recreated in absolute detail. The environments were not separated by walls but by unseen force fields, each environment phasing tastefully into another. Most of the fluctuants were not indigenous to Earth at any period in her history (save for a few primitive chameleons, offapeckers, and the like) but were drawn from many distant planets beyond the Solar System. Virtually all were intelligent, especially the mimics.

As the three people walked through the various environments, protected from attack by their own force shields, creature after creature encountered them and changed shape, mimicking crudely or perfectly either Jherek, or Jagged, or Mongrove. Some changed shape so swiftly (from Jagged, say, to Mongrove, to Jherek) that Jherek himself began to feel quite strange.

The Human House was next and it was in this that Jherek hoped to find the woman he intended to love.

The Human House was the largest in the menagerie and whereas many of the other houses were stocked from different areas of space, this was stocked from different ages in Earth's history. The house stretched for several square miles and, like the Fluctuant House, its environments were phased into each other (in chronological order), recreating different habitats from many periods. In the broader categories were represented Neanderthal Man, Piltdown Man, Religious Man and Scientific Man and there were, of course, many sub-divisions.

'I have here,' said Mongrove, almost animatedly, 'men and women from virtually every major period in our history.'

He paused. 'Have you, my friends, any particular interest? The Phradracean Tyrannies, possibly?' He indicated the environment in which they now stood. The houses were square, sandy blocks, standing on a sand-coloured concrete. The representative of this age was wearing a garment (if it was a garment) of similar material and colour, also square. His head and limbs projected rather incongruously from it and he looked a comical sight as he walked about shouting at the three men in his own language and waving his fists. He nonetheless kept a safe distance.

'He seems angry,' said Lord Jagged, watching him with quizzical amusement.

'It was an angry age,' said Mongrove. 'Like so many.'

44

They passed through that environment and through several more before Mongrove stopped again.

'Or the glorious Irish Empire,' he said. 'Five hundred years of the most marvellous Celtic Twilight covering forty planets. This is the guinness, or ruler, himself.'

They were in an environment of lush green grass and soft light in which stood a two-storey building in wood and stone with a sign hanging from it. Outside the building, on a wooden bench, sat a handsome, red-faced individual dressed in a rather strange dun-coloured garment which was belted tightly at the waist and had a collar turned up to shade the face. On the head was a soft brown hat with a brim turned down over the eyes. In one hand was a pot of dark liquid on which floated a thick, white scum. The man raised this pot frequently to his lips and drained it, whereupon it instantly filled again, to the man's constant, smiling delight. He sang all the time, too, a lugubrious dirge-like melody, which seemed to please him, though sometimes he would lower his head and weep.

'He can be so sad,' said Mongrove admiringly. 'He laughs, he sings, but the sadness fills him. He is one of my favourites.'

They moved on, through examples of the prehistoric Greek Golden Age, the British Renaissance, the Corinian Republican era, the Imperial American Confederation, the Mexican Overlordship, The Yulinish Emperors, the Twelve Planet Union, the Thirty Planet Union, the Anarchic States, The Cool Theocracy, the Dark Green Council, the Farajite Warlord period, the Herodian Empire, the Gienic Empire, the Sugar Dictatorship, the Sonic Assassination period, the time of the Invisible Mark (most peculiar of many similar periods), the Rope Girl age, the First, Second and Third Paternalisms, the Ship Cultures, the Engineering Millennium, the age of the Planet Builders, and hundreds more.

And all the time Jherek looked about him for a sign of the grey time-traveller while, mechanically, he praised Mongrove's collection, leaving most of the expressions of awe and delight to Lord Jagged, who deliberately drew attention away from Jherek.

And yet it was Mongrove who pointed her out first as they entered an environment somewhat barer than the rest.

'And here is the latest addition to my collection. I'm very proud to have acquired her, but as yet she will not tell me what to build so that she may be happy in a habitat which suits her best.'

Jherek turned and looked full into the face of the grey time-traveller.

She was glaring. She was red with rage. At first Jherek did not realise that he was the object of that rage. He thought that when she recognised him, when she saw what he was wearing, her expression would soften.

But it grew harder.

'Has she had a translation pill yet?' he asked of Mongrove. But Mongrove was staring at him with a tinge of suspicion.

'Your costumes are very similar, Jherek.'

'Yes,' said Jherek. 'I have already met the time-traveller. Last night. At the Duke of Queens'. I was so impressed by the costume that I made one for myself.'

'I see.' Mongrove's brow cleared a little.

'But what a coincidence,' said Lord Jagged briskly. 'We had no idea she was in *your* collection, Lord Mongrove. How extraordinary.'

'Yes,' said Mongrove quietly.

Jherek cleared his throat.

'I wonder . . .' began Mongrove.

Jherek turned to address the lady, making a low bow and saying courteously: 'I trust you are well, madam, and that you can now understand me better.'

'Understand! Understand!' The lady's voice was hysterical. She did not seem at all flattered. 'I understand you to be a depraved, disgusting, corrupt and abominable *thing*, sir!'

Some of the words still meant nothing to Jherek. He smiled politely. 'Perhaps another translation pill would . . .'

'You are the foulest creature I have ever encountered in my entire life,' said the lady. 'And now I am convinced that I have died and am in a more horrible Hell than any that Man could imagine. Oh, my sins must have been terrible when I lived.'

'Hell?' said Mongrove, his interest awakened. 'Are you from Hell?'

'Is that another name for the 19th century?' asked Lord Jagged. He seemed amused.

'There is much I can learn from you,' said Mongrove eagerly. 'How glad I am that it was I who claimed you.'

'What is your name?' said Jherek wildly, completely taken aback by her reaction.

She drew herself up, her lip curling in disdain as she eyed him from head to toe.

'My name, sir is Mrs Amelia Underwood and, if this is not Hell, but some dreadful foreign land, I demand that I be allowed to speak to the British Consul at once!'

Jherek looked up at Mongrove and Mongrove looked down in astonishment at Jherek.

'She is one of the strangest I have ever acquired,' said Mongrove.

'I will take her off your hands,' said Jherek.

'No, no,' said Mongrove, 'though the thought is kind. No, I think I will enjoy studying her.' He turned his attention back to Mrs Underwood, speaking politely. 'How hot would you like the flames?'

CHAPTER SIX

A PLEASING MEETING: THE IRON ORCHID
DEVISES A SCHEME

HAVING successfully convinced melancholy Mongrove that flames would not be the best environment for the grey time-traveller and having made one or two alternative suggestions based on his own detailed knowledge of the period, Jherek decided that it was time to offer his adieux. Mongrove was still inclined to dart at him the odd suspicious glance; Mrs Amelia Underwood was plainly in no mood at the moment to receive his declarations of love and, it seemed to him, Lord Jagged was becoming bored and wanting to leave.

Mongrove escorted them from the Human House and back to where the gold and ebony locomotive awaited them, its colours clashing horribly with the blacks, dark greens and muddy browns of Mongrove's lair.

'Well,' said Mongrove, 'thank you for your advice, Jherek. I think my new specimen should settle down soon. Of course, some creatures are inclined to pine, no matter how much care you take of them. Some die and have to be resurrected and sent back to where they come from.'

'If there's any further help I can give . . .' murmured Jherek anxiously, horrified at the idea.

'I shall ask for it, of course.' There was perhaps a trace of coolness in Mongrove's tone.

'Or if I can spend some time with . . .'

'You have been,' said Lord Jagged of Canaria, posing above them on the footplate, 'a gracious host, and gigantic, Mongrove, in your generosity. I'll remember how much you would like to add that gloomy space-traveller to your collection. I'll try to acquire him for you in some way. Would you, incidentally, be interested in making a trade?'

'A trade?' Mongrove shrugged. 'Yes, why not? But for what? What have I worth offering?'

'Oh, I thought I'd take the 19th century specimen off your hands,' Jagged said airily. 'I honestly don't think you'll have much joy from it. Also, there is someone to whom it would make a suitable gift.'

'Jherek?' Mongrove was alert. 'Is that whom you mean?' He turned his huge head to look soulfully at Jherek, who was pretending that he hadn't been listening to the conversation.

'Ah, now,' said Lord Jagged, 'that would not be tactful, would it, Mongrove, to reveal?'

'I suppose it wouldn't.' Mongrove gave a great sniff. The rain ran down his face and soaked his dull, shapeless garments. 'But you would never get My Lady Charlotina to give up her alien. So there is no point to this discussion.'

'It might be possible,' said Lord Jagged. The lizard circlet on his head hissed its complaint at the soaking it was receiving. He ducked back into the cabin of the locomotive. 'Are you coming, Jherek?'

Jherek bowed to Mongrove. 'You have been very kind, Mongrove. I am glad we understand each other better now.'

Mongrove's eyes narrowed as he watched Jherek drift up to the footplate. 'Yes,' said the giant, 'I am glad of that, too, Jherek.'

'And you will be pleased to make the trade?' said Jagged. 'If I can bring you the alien?'

Mongrove pursed his enormous lips. 'If you *can* bring me the alien, you may have the time-traveller.'

'It's a bargain!' said Lord Jagged gaily. 'I shall bring him to you shortly.'

And at last Mongrove found it in himself to voice his suspicions. 'Lord Jagged. Did you come here with the specific desire to acquire my new specimen?'

Lord Jagged laughed. 'So that is why your manner has seemed reserved! It was bothering me, Mongrove, for I felt I had offended you in some way.'

'But is that the reason?' Mongrove continued insistently. He turned to Jherek. 'Have you been deceiving me, pretending to be my friends, while all the time it was your intention to take my specimen away from me?'

'I am shocked!'

Lord Jagged drew himself up in a swirl of draperies.

'Shocked, Mongrove.'

Jherek could not restrain a grin as he marvelled at Lord Jagged's histrionic powers. But then Lord Jagged turned his grim frown upon Jherek, too.

'And why do you smile, Jherek Carnelian? Do you believe Mongrove? Do you think that I brought you with me on a mere pretence—that my intention was *not* to heal the rift between you?'

'No,' said Jherek, casting down his eyes and trying to rid himself of the unwelcome grin. 'I am sorry, Lord Jagged.'

'And I am sorry, too.' Mongrove's lips trembled. 'I have wronged you both. Forgive me.'

'Of course, most miserable of Mongroves,' said Lord Jagged kindly. 'Of course! Of course! Of course! You were right to be suspicious. Your collection is the envy of the planet. Each one of your specimens is a gem. *Remain* cautious! There are others, less scrupulous than myself or Jherek Carnelian, who *would* deceive you.'

'How unkind I have been. How ungenerous. How ill-mannered. How mean-spirited!' Mongrove groaned. 'What a wretch I am, Lord Jagged. Now I hate myself. And now you see me for what I am, you will despise me forever!'

'Despise? Never! Your prudence is admirable. I admire it. I admire you. And now, dearest Mongrove, we must leave. Perhaps I will return with the specimen you desire. In a day or so.'

'You are more than gracious. Farewell, Lord Jagged. Farewell, Jherek. Please feel free to visit me whenever you wish. Though I realise I am poor company and that therefore you will have little inclination to . . .'

'Farewell, weeping Mongrove!' Jherek pulled the whistle and the train made a mournful noise—a kind of despairing honk—before it began to ascend slowly into the drooping day.

Lord Jagged had resumed his position on the couch. His eyes were closed, his face expressionless. Jherek turned from where he stood looking through the observation window. 'Lord Jagged, you are a model of deviousness.'

'Come now, my cunning Carnelian,' murmured Lord Jagged, his eyes still shut, 'you, too, show a fine talent in that direction.'

'Poor Mongrove. How neatly his suspicion was turned.' Jherek sat down beside his friend. 'But how are we to acquire Mrs Amelia Underwood? The Lady Charlotina might not hate Mongrove, but she is jealous of her treasures. She will not give the little alien to us.'

'Then we must *steal* him, eh?' Jagged opened his pale eyes and there was a mischievous ecstasy shining from them. 'We shall be *thieves*, Jherek, you and I.'

The idea was so astonishing that it took Jherek a while to understand its implications. And then he laughed in delight. 'You are so inventive, Lord Jagged! And it fits so well!'

'It does. Mad with love, you will go to any lengths to have possession of the object of that love. All other considerations—friendship, prestige, dignity—are swept aside. I see you like it.' Lord Jagged put a slender finger to his lips, which now bore just a trace of a smile. 'What a succulent drama we are beginning to build. Ah, Jherek, my dear, you were *born*—for *love!*'

'Hm,' said Jherek, without rancour, 'I am beginning to suspect that I was born so that you might be supplied with raw materials with which to exercise your own considerable literary gifts, my lord.'

'You flatter, flatter, *flatter* me!'

Later a voice spoke gently in Jherek's ear. 'My son, my ruby! Is that your aircar?'

Jherek recognised the voice of the Iron Orchid. 'Yes, mother, it is. And where are you?'

'Below you, dear.'

He got up and looked down. On a chequered landscape of blue, purple and yellow, flat, save for a few crystal trees dotted here and there, he could make out two figures. He looked at Jagged. 'Do you mind if we pause a while?'

'Not at all.'

Jherek ordered the locomotive to descend and was standing on the footplate by the time it landed in one of the orange squares, measuring about twelve feet across and made of tightly packed tiny shamrocks. In the neighbouring square, a green one, sat the Iron Orchid with Li Pao upon her knee. Even as Jherek lowered himself from his car the colours of the squares changed again.

'I just can't make up my mind, today,' she explained. 'Can you help me, Jherek?'

She had always had a predilection for fur and now a fine, golden down covered her body, save for her face which she had coloured to match Li Pao's. Li Pao wore the same blue overalls as usual and seemed embarrassed. He tried to get off the Iron Orchid's furry knee, but she held him firmly. She was seated in a beautiful, shimmering force chair. Bluebirds wheeled and dipped just above her head.

The chequered plain stretched away for a mile on all sides. Jherek contemplated it. His mind was occupied with other matters and he found it difficult to offer advice. At last he said: 'I think any arrangement that you make is perfect, most ornamental of Orchids. Good afternoon, Li Pao.'

'Good afternoon,' said Li Pao rather distantly. Although a member of the Duke of Queens' menagerie, he chose to wander abroad most of the time. Jherek thought that Li Pao didn't really like the austere environment which the Duke of Queens had created for him, though Li Pao claimed that it was all he really needed. Li Pao looked beyond Jherek. 'I see you have your decadent friend, Lord Jagged, with you.'

Lord Jagged acknowledged Li Pao with a bow that set all his lilac robes a-flutter and made the living lizard rear upon his brow and snap its teeth. Then Lord Jagged took one of the Iron Orchid's fur-covered hands and pressed it to his lips. 'Softest of beasts,' he murmured. He stroked her shoulder. 'Prettiest of pelts.'

Li Pao got up. He was sulking. He stood some distance off and pretended an interest in a crystal tree. The Iron Orchid laughed, her hand encircling the back of Lord Jagged's neck and pulling his head down to kiss his lizard upon its serrated snout.

Leaving them to their ritual, Jherek joined Li Pao beside the tree. 'We have just returned from Mongrove's. Aren't you a friend of his?'

Li Pao nodded. 'Something of a friend. We have one or two ideas in common. But I suspect that Mongrove's views are not always his own. Not always sincere.'

'Mongrove? There is nobody less insincere.'

'In this world? Perhaps not. But the fact remains . . .' Li Pao flicked a silver crystal fruit and it emitted a single pure, sweet note for two seconds before falling silent again. 'I mean, it is not a great deal to say of someone native to your society.'

'Aha!' said Jherek portentously. He had not actually been listening. 'I have tumbled, Li Pao, in love,' he announced. 'I am desperately in love—mindlessly in love—with a girl.'

'You don't know the meaning of love,' Li Pao replied dismissively. 'Love involves dedication, self-denial, nobility of temperament. All of them qualities which you people no longer possess. Is this another of your frightful travesties? Why are you dressed like that? What ghosts you are. What pathetic fantasies you pursue. You play mindless games, without purpose or meaning, while the universe dies around you.'

'I am sure that's true,' said Jherek politely. 'But if it is, Li Pao, why do you not return to your own time? It is difficult, but not impossible.'

'It is virtually impossible. You must surely have heard of the Morphail Effect. One can go back in time, certainly—perhaps for a few minutes at most. No scientist in the Earth's long history has ever been able to solve that problem. But—even if there was a good chance of my remaining there once I *had* returned—what could I tell my people? That all their work, their self-sacrifice, their idealism, their establishment of justice, finally led to the creation of your putrid world? I would be a monster if I tried. Would I describe your overripe and rotting technologies, your foul sexual practices, your degenerate bourgeois pastimes at which you idle away the centuries? No!'

Li Pao's eyes shone as he warmed to his theme and felt the full power of his own heroism surging through him.

'No! It is my lot to remain a prisoner here. My self-appointed lot. My sacrifice. It is my duty to warn you of the consequences of your decadent behaviour. My duty to try to steer you on to straighter paths, to consider more serious matters, before it is too late!' He paused, panting and proud.

'And meanwhile,' came the languid tones of the Iron Orchid as she approached, hanging on to the arm of Lord Jagged who raised a complimentary eyebrow at Li Pao, 'it is also your lot, Li Pao, to entertain your Orchid, to pleasure her, to adore her (as I know you do) and, most caustic of critics, to sweeten her days with your fine displays of emotion.'

'Oh, you are wicked! You are imperialistic! You are vile!'

Li Pao stalked away.

'But mark my words,' he said over his shoulder, 'the apocalypse is not that far away. You will wish, Iron Orchid, that you had not made sport of me.'

'What dark, dark hints! Does Li Pao love you?' asked Lord Jagged. There was a speculative expression on his white features. He glanced sardonically at Jherek. 'Perhaps he can teach you a few responses, my novice?'

'Perhaps.' Jherek yawned. The strain of his visit to Mongrove had tired him a bit.

'Why?' The Iron Orchid stared with interest at her son. 'Are you learning "jealousy" now, blood of my blood? Instead of virtue? Isn't jealousy what Li Pao is doing now?'

Jherek had forgotten his craze of the day before.

'I believe so,' he replied. 'Perhaps I should cultivate Li Pao. Isn't jealousy one of the components of true love, Lord Jagged?'

'You know more of the details of the period than I, joyful Jherek. All I have helped you do is to put them into a *context*.'

'And a splendid context, too,' Jherek added. He looked after the departing Li Pao.

'Come now, Jherek,' said his mother, laying down her sleekness upon a padded couch and dismissing the chequered field (it *had* been awful, thought Jherek). The field became a desert. The blue-birds became eagles. Not far off a clump of palms sprang up beside a waterhole. The Iron Orchid pretended not to notice that the oasis had appeared directly beneath where Li Pao had been standing. The Chinese was now glowering at her. All that could be seen above the surface of the water was his head. 'What,' she continued, 'is this game you and Lord Jagged have invented?'

'Mother, I'm in love with such a wonderful girl,' began Jherek.

'Ah!' She sighed with delight.

'My heart sings when I see her, mother. My pulse throbs when I think of her. My life means nothing when she's not there.'

'Charming!'

'And, dear mother, she is everything that a girl should be. She's beautiful, intelligent, understanding, imaginative, cruel. And, mother, I mean to *marry* her!'

Exhausted by his performance, Jherek fell back upon the sand.

The Iron Orchid clapped her hands enthusiastically. It was a some-what muffled clap, because of the fur.

'Admirable!' She blew him a kiss. 'Jherek, my doll, you are a *genius!* No other description will do!' She leaned forward. 'Now. The background?'

And Jherek explained all that had happened since he had last seen his mother, and all that he and Jagged had planned—including the Theft.

'Luscious,' she said. 'So we must somehow steal the dreary alien from My Lady Charlotina. She'd never give it away. I know her.

54

You're right. A difficult task.' She looked at the oasis, crying petulantly: 'Oh, Li Pao, *do* come out of there.'

Li Pao scowled across the water. He refused to speak. His body remained submerged.

'That's why I'm so attached to him, really,' the Iron Orchid explained. 'He sulks so prettily.' She rested her chin upon her furry fist and considered the problem at hand.

Jherek looked about him, contemplating the enterprise afresh and wondering if it were not becoming too complicated. Too boring, even. Perhaps he should invent a simpler affectation. Being in love took up so much *time*.

At last the Iron Orchid looked up. 'The first thing we must do is visit My Lady Charlotina. A large group of us. As many as possible. We shall make merry. The party will be exciting, confused. While it is at its height, we steal the alien. We shall have to decide the actual method of theft when we are there. I don't remember how her menagerie is arranged, and anyway it has probably changed since I visited her last. What do you think, Jagged?'

'I think that you are the genius, my blossom, from which this genius sprang.' Grinning, Lord Jagged put his arm around Jherek's grey-clad shoulders. 'Most fragrant of flowers, it is an excellent notion. But none should be aware of our true intent. We three alone shall plan the robbery. The others will, unknowingly, cover our attempt. Do you agree, Jherek?'

'I agree. What a complimentary pair you are. You praise me for your own cleverness. You credit me with your inventiveness. I—I am merely your tool.'

'Nonsense.' Lord Jagged closed his eyes as if in modesty. 'You sketch out the grand design. We are merely your pupils—we block out the less interesting details of the canvas.'

The Iron Orchid stretched out her paw to stroke Lord Jagged's lizard, which had become dormant and was almost asleep. 'Our friends must be fired with the idea of visiting My Lady Charlotina. We can only *trust* that she is at home. *And* that she welcomes us. Then,' she laughed her delicate laugh, 'we must hope we are not detected in our deceit. Before the theft's accomplished, at least. And the *consequences!* Can you imagine the complications which are bound to arise? You remember, Jherek, we were hoping for another series of events to rival that which followed Flags?'

'This should easily rival Flags,' said Lord Jagged. 'It makes me feel young again.'

'Were you ever *young*, Jagged?' asked the Iron Orchid in surprise.

'Well, you know what I mean,' he said.

CHAPTER SEVEN

TO STEAL A SPACE-TRAVELLER

My Lady Charlotina had always preferred the subterranean existence.

Her territory of Below-the-Lake was not merely subterranean, it was subaqueous, too, in the truest sense. It was made up of mile upon mile of high, muggy caverns linked by tunnels and smaller caves, into which one might put whole cities and towns without difficulty. My Lady Charlotina had hollowed the whole place out herself, many years before, under the bed and following the contours of one of the few permanent lakes left on the planet.

This lake, was, of course, Lake Billy the Kid.

Lake Billy the Kid was named after the legendary American explorer, astronaut and bon-vivant, who had been crucified around the year 2000 because it was discovered that he possessed the hindquarters of a goat. In Billy the Kid's time such permutations were apparently not fashionable.

Lake Billy the Kid was perhaps the most ancient landmark in the world. It had been moved only twice in the past fifty thousand years.

At Below-the-Lake, the revels were in full swing.

A hundred or so of My Lady Charlotina's closest friends had arrived to entertain their delighted (if surprised) hostess and themselves. The party was noisy. It was chaotic.

Jherek Carnelian had had no difficulty, in this atmosphere, in slipping away to the menagerie and at last discovering My Lady Charlotina's latest acquisition in one of the two or three thousand smaller caverns she used to house her specimens.

The cavern containing Yusharisp's environment was between one containing a flickering, hissing flame-creature (which had been discovered on the Sun but had probably originally come from another star altogether) and another containing a microscopic dog-like alien from nearby Betelgeux.

Yusharisp's environment was rather dark and chilly. Its main feature was a pulsing, squeaking black and purple tower which was covered in a most unappealing kind of mould. The tower was doubtless what Yusharisp lived in on his home planet. Apart from the tower there was a profusion of drooping grey plants and jagged dark yellow rocks. The tower resembled the spaceship which My Lady Charlotina had had to disseminate (if it *had* disseminated, as such, being of unearthly origin).

Yusharisp sat on a rock outside his tower, his four little legs folded under his spherical body. Most of his eyes were closed, save one at the front and one at the back. He seemed lost in sullen thoughts and did not notice Jherek at first. Jherek adjusted one of his rings, broke the force-barrier for a second, and walked through.

'You're Yusharisp, aren't you?' said Jherek. 'I came to say how interested I was in your speech of the other day.'

All Yusharisp's eyes opened round his head. His body swayed a little so that for a moment Jherek thought it would roll off and bounce over the ground like a ball. Yusharisp's many eyes were filled with gloom. 'You, skree, responded to it?' he said in a small, despairing voice.

'It was very pleasant,' said Jherek vaguely, thinking that perhaps he had begun on the wrong tack. 'Very pleasant indeed.'

'Pleasant? Now I am completely confused.' Yusharisp began to rise on the rock upon his four little legs. 'You found what I had to say *pleasant?*'

Jherek realised he had not said the right thing. 'I meant,' he went on, 'that it was pleasant to hear such sentiments expressed.' He racked his brains to remember exactly what the alien had said. He knew the general drift of it. He had heard it many times before. It had been about the end of the universe or the end of the galaxy, or something like that. Very similar in tone to a lot of what Li Pao had to say. Was it because the people on Earth were not living according to the principles and customs currently fashionable on the alien's home planet? That was the usual message: 'You do not live like us. Therefore you are going to die. It is inevitable. And it will be your own fault.'

'Refreshing, I meant,' said Jherek lamely.

'I see, skree, what you mean, skree.' Mollified, the alien hopped from the rock and stood quite close to Jherek, his front row of eyes staring roundly up into Jherek's face.

'I am pleased that there are *some* serious-minded people on this planet,' Yusharisp continued. 'In all my travels I have never had such a reception. Most beings have been moved and (roar) saddened by my news. Some have accepted it with dignity, skree, and calm. Some have been angry or disbelieving, even attacked me. Some have not been moved at all, for death holds no fears for, skree, them. But, skree, on Earth (roar) I have been *imprisoned* and my spaceship has quite casually been *destroyed!* And no one has expressed regret, anger—anything but—what?—amusement. As if what I had to say was a joke. They do not take me seriously, yet they lock me in this cell as if I had, skree, committed some kind of crime (roar)! Can you explain?'

'Oh, yes,' said Jherek. 'My Lady Charlotina wanted you for her collection. You see, she hasn't got a space-traveller of your shape and size.'

'Collection? This is a (roar) *zoo*, skree, then?'

'Of sorts. She hasn't explained? She can be a bit vague, My Lady Charlotina, I agree. But she *has* made you comfortable. Your own environment in all its details.'

Jherek looked without enthusiasm at the drooping plants and dark yellow rocks, the mouldy tower sticking up into the chill air. It was easy to see why the alien had chosen to leave. 'Nice.'

Yusharisp turned away and began to waddle towards his tower. 'It is useless. My translator is malfunctioning more than I realised. I cannot transmit my message properly. It is my fault, not yours. I deserve this.'

'What exactly was the message,' said Jherek. He saw a chance to find out without appearing to have forgotten. 'Perhaps if you could repeat it I could tell you if I understood.'

The alien appeared to brighten and walk backwards. The only difference between his back and his front, as far as Jherek could see, was that his mouth was in the front. The eyes looked exactly the same. He swivelled round so that his mouth aperture faced Jherek.

'Well,' Yusharisp began, 'basically what has happened is that the universe, having ceased to expand, is contracting. Our researches have shown that this is what always happens—expansion/contraction, expansion/contraction, expansion/contraction—the universe forming and re-forming all the time. Perhaps that formation is always the same—each cycle being more or less a repeat of the previous one—I don't know. Anyway that takes us into the realm of Time, not Space, and I know nothing at all of Time.'

'An interesting theory,' said Jherek, who found it somewhat boring.

'It is not a theory.'

'Aha.'

'The universe has begun to contract. As a result, skree, all matter not in a completely gaseous (roar) state already, will be destroyed as it is pulled into what you might call the central vortex of the universe. My own, skree, planet has already gone by now, I should think.' The alien sighed a deep sigh. 'It's a matter of millennia, perhaps even less time than that, before your galaxy goes the same way.'

'There, there.' Jherek patted the alien on the top part of its body. Yusharisp looked up, offended.

'This is (roar) no time for sexual advances, skree, my friend!'

Jherek took his hand away. 'My apologies.'

'At another time, perhaps . . .' Yusharisp's translator growled and moaned and he kept clearing his throat until it had stopped. 'I am, I must admit, rather dispirited,' he said. 'A trifle on (roar) edge, as you might expect.'

Jherek's plan (or at least an important part of it) now crystallised. He said:

'That is why I intend to help you escape from My Lady Charlotina's menagerie.'

'You do? But the force-field and so on? The security must be, skree, very tight.'

Jherek did not tell the alien that he could, if he wished, wander at large across the whole planet. The only intelligent creatures who remained in menageries remained there because they desired it. Jherek reasoned that it was best, for his purposes, if Yusharisp really did think he was a prisoner.

'I can deal with all that,' he said airily.

'I am deeply grateful to you.' One of the alien's brown, bandy legs rose and touched Jherek on the thigh. 'I could not believe that *every* creature on this planet could be so, skree, skree, inhumane. But my spaceship? How will I escape from your world to continue my journey, to carry my message?'

'We'll cope with that problem later,' Jherek assured him.

'Very, skree, well. I understand. You are risking so much already.' The alien hopped eagerly about on his four legs. 'Can we leave now? Or must secret preparations be made, skree?'

'The important thing is that you shouldn't be detected leaving by My Lady Charlotina,' Jherek answered. 'Therefore I must ask you if you will object to a little restructuring. Temporary, of course. And not very sophisticated—there isn't time. I'll put you back to your original form before we get to Mongrove's . . .'

'Mon(roar)grove's?'

'Our, um, hideout. A friend. A sympathiser.'

'And what, skree, is "restructuring"?' Yusharisp's manner had become suspicious.

'A disguise,' said Jherek. 'I must alter your body.'

'A skree—a skree—a skree—a *trick*. Another cruel trick! (roar)' The alien became agitated and made as if to run into his tower. Jherek could see why Mongrove had seen a fellow spirit in Yusharisp. They would get on splendidly.

'Not a trick upon you. Upon the woman who has imprisoned you here.'

Yusharisp calmed down, but a score of his eyes were darting from side to side, crossing in an alarming manner.

'And what (roar) then? Where will you take, skree, me?'

'To Mongrove's. He sympathises with your plight. He wishes to listen to all you have to say. He is perhaps the one person on the planet (apart, of course, from myself) who really understands what you are trying to do.'

Perhaps, thought Jherek, he was not deceiving the alien, after all. It was quite likely that Mongrove would want to help Yusharisp when he heard the whole of the little fellow's story. 'Now——' Jherek fiddled with one of his rings. 'If you will allow me . . .'

'Very well,' said the alien, seeming to slump in resignation. 'After all, there is, skree, nothing more (roar) to lose, is there?'

'Jherek! Sweet child. Child of nature. Son of the Earth! Over here!'

My Lady Charlotina, surrounded by many of her guests, including the Iron Orchid and Lord Jagged of Canaria (who were both working hard to keep her attention) waved to Jherek.

Jherek and Yusharisp (his body restructured to resemble that of an apeman) moved through a throng of laughing guests in one of the main caverns, close to the Gateway in the Water through which Jherek hoped to make his escape.

This cavern had glowing golden walls and a roof and floor of mirrored silver so that it seemed that everything took place simultaneously a hundred times upon the floor and the ceiling of the cavern. My Lady Charlotina floated in a force-hammock while the dwarfish scientist, Brannart Morphail, lay gasping between her knees. Morphail was perhaps the last true scientist on Earth, experimenting in the only possible field left for such a person—the field of time-manipulation. Morphail raised his head as My Lady Charlotina signalled Jherek. Morphail peered through ragged tufts of white, yellow and blue hair. He licked red lips surrounded by a tattered beard of orange and black. His dark eyes glowered, as if he blamed Jherek for the interrupted intercourse.

Jherek had to acknowledge her. He bowed, smiled and tried to think of some polite phrase on which to leave.

My Lady Charlotina was naked. All four of her latest breasts were tinted gold with silver nipples to match her cavern's décor. Her body was rose-pink and radiated softness and comfort. Her long, thin face, with its sharp nose and pointed chin, was embroidered in threads of scintillating light-thread which shifted colour constantly and sometimes appeared to alter the whole outline of her features.

Jherek, with the alien clinging nervously to him with one of its feet, tried to move on but then had to pause to instruct the alien, in a whisper, to use one of the upper appendages if it wished to hold to him at all. He was afraid My Lady Charlotina had already detected his theft.

Yusharisp looked as if he were about to bolt now. Jherek laid a restraining hand on the alien's new body.

'Who is that with you?'

My Lady Charlotina's embroidered face was, for a moment, scarlet all over.

'Is that a time-traveller?' Her force-hammock began to drift towards Jherek and Yusharisp. The sudden motion threw Brannart Morphail to the floor of the cavern. Moodily, he lay where he had fallen, looking at himself in the mirrored surface and refusing the proffered hands of both Lord Jagged of Canaria and the Iron Orchid. They stood near him, trying not to look at Jherek who, in turn, tried to ignore them. An exchange of glances at this stage might easily make My Lady Charlotina that much more suspicious.

'Yes,' said Jherek quickly. 'A time-traveller.'

At this, Brannart Morphail looked up.

'He recently arrived. I found him. He'll be the basis of what will be my new collection.'

'Oh, so you are to vie with me? I must watch you, Jherek. You're so *clever*.'

'Yes, you must watch. My collection, though, will never match yours, my charming Charlotina.'

'Have you seen my new space-traveller?' She cast her eyes over the alien as she spoke.

'Yes. Yesterday, I think. Or the day before. Very fine.'

'Thank you. This *is* an odd specimen. Are you sure it's genuine, dear?'

'Oh, yes. Absolutely.'

Jherek had given him the form of a pre-10th century, or Piltdown, Man. He was apelike, somewhat shaggy and inclined (because of Yusharisp's normal method of perambulation) to drop to all fours. He was dressed in animal skins and (an authentic touch) carried a pistol (a club with a metal handle and a blunt, wooden end).

'He didn't, surely, come in his own machine?' said My Lady Charlotina.

Jherek looked about for his mother and Lord Jagged, but both had slipped away. Only Brannart Morphail was left, slowly rising from the floor.

'No,' said Jherek. 'A machine from some other age must have brought him. A temporal accident no doubt. Some poor time-traveller plunged into the past, dragged back to his present without his machine. The primitive gets in, pushes a button or two and— heigh-ho—here he is!'

'He told you this, juicy Jherek?'

'Speculation. He is, of course, not intelligent, as we understand it. An interesting mixture of human and animal, though.'

'Can he speak?'

'In grunts,' said Jherek, nodding furiously for no real reason.

'He can communicate in grunts.' He looked hard at the alien, warning him not to speak. The alien was a fool. He could easily ruin the whole thing. But Yusharisp remained silent.

'What a shame. Well, it's a *start* to a collection, I suppose, dear,' she added kindly.

Brannart Morphail was now on his feet. He hobbled over to join them. He did not need to have a hump-back and a club-foot, but he was a traditionalist in almost everything and he knew that once all true scientists had looked as he did now. He was touchily proud of his appearance and had not changed it for centuries.

'What machine did he come in?' queried Brannart Morphail. 'I ask because it could not be one of the four or five basic kinds which have been invented and re-invented through the course of our history.'

'And why could it not be?' Jherek was beginning to feel disturbed. Morphail knew everything there was to know about time. Perhaps he should have concocted a slightly better story. Still, it was too late now to change it.

'Because I should have detected it in my laboratories. My scanners are constantly checking the chronowaves. Any object such as a time machine is immediately registered on its arrival in our time.'

'Ah.' Jherek was at a loss for an explanation.

'So I should like to see the time machine in which your specimen arrived,' said Brannart Morphail. 'It must be a new type. To us, that is.'

'Tomorrow,' said Jherek Carnelian wildly, guiding his charge forward and away from My Lady Charlotina and Brannart Morphail. 'You must visit me tomorrow.'

'I will.'

'Jherek. Are you *leaving* my party?' My Lady Charlotina seemed offended. 'After all, weren't you one of the people who thought of it? Really, my tulip, you should stay a little longer.'

'I am sorry.' Jherek felt trapped. He adjusted the animal skin to cover as much of Yusharisp's body as possible. He had not had time to adjust the skin colour, which was still pretty much the same, a muddy brown with green fleck in it. 'You see, my specimen must be, um, fed.'

'Fed? We can feed him here.'

'Special food,' said Jherek. 'Only I know the recipe.'

'But we *pride* ourselves on our cuisine at my menagerie,' said My

Lady Charlotina. 'Let me know what he eats and it shall be prepared instantly.'

'Oh,' said Jherek.

My Lady Charlotina laughed and her embroidery went through a sudden and startling series of colours. 'Jherek. You are looking positively *shifty*. What on earth are you planning?'

'Planning? Nothing.' He felt miserable and wished deeply that he had not embarked upon this scheme.

'Your time-traveller. Did you really acquire him as you said, or is there some secret? Have you been back in time yourself?'

'No. No.' His lips were dry. He adjusted his body moisture. It didn't seem to make much difference.

'Or did you make the time-traveller yourself, as I suspected? Could he be a fake?'

She was getting altogether too close. Jherek fixed his eye on the exit and murmured to Yusharisp. 'That is the way to freedom. We must . . .'

My Lady Charlotina drifted closer, bent forward to peer at the disguised alien. Her perfume was so strong that Jherek felt faint. She addressed Yusharisp, her eyes narrowing:

'What's your name?' she said.

'He doesn't speak——' Jherek's voice cracked.

'Skree,' said Yusharisp.

'His name is Skree,' said Jherek, pushing the space-traveller forward with the flat of his hand. The space-traveller fell forward and, upon all fours, began to skitter in the direction of one of several tunnels leading from the cavern. His club lay gleaming on the floor behind him.

Lady Charlotina's brows drew closer together as an expression of dawning suspicion gradually spread over her embroidered face.

'I'll see you tomorrow, then,' said Brannart Morphail briskly, unaware of any other level of conversation taking place. 'About the time machine.' He turned to My Lady Charlotina, who had risen on one elbow in her force-hammock and was staring, open-mouthed, as Jherek sped away after the alien.

'Exciting,' said Brannart Morphail. 'A new form of time-travel, evidently.'

'Or a new form of affectation,' said My Lady Charlotina grimly. However, her voice was more melodramatic than sincere as she called, on a fading note: 'Jherek! Jherek!'

Jherek kept running. But he turned, shouting: 'My alien—I mean my time-traveller—he's escaping. Must catch him. Wonderful party. Farewell, coruscating Charlotina, for now!'

'Oh, oh, Jherek!'

And he fled after Yusharisp, through the tunnels to the Gateway in the Water—a tube of energy pushed up from the bottom of the lake to the surface—and thence to where his little locomotive hovered, awaiting him.

Jherek shot into the sky, dragging the alien (who had no antigravity ring) with him.

'Into the aircar!' Jherek panted, floating towards the locomotive.

Together they tumbled in and collapsed on the plush and ermine couch.

Jherek pulled the whistle cord.

'Mongrove's,' he said, watching the lake for signs of pursuit, 'and speedily.'

With a wild hoot, the locomotive chugged rapidly towards the East, letting out great clouds of scarlet steam.

Looking back and down Jherek saw My Lady Charlotina emerge with a gush from the shimmering lake and, still in her force-hammock, still raised on one elbow, shout after him as he disappeared into the evening sky.

Jherek strained to catch the words, for she was using no form of projection. He hoped, too, she would be sporting enough not to use any kind of tracer on his aircar, or a traction beam to haul him back to Below-the-Lake. Possibly she still didn't realise what he had done. But he heard the words clearly enough. 'Stop,' she called theatrically, languidly. 'Stop thief!'

And Jherek felt his legs grow weak. He experienced one of the most exquisite thrills of his entire life. Even certain experiences of his adolescence hadn't done this for him. He sighed with pleasure.

'Stop,' he murmured to himself as the locomotive moved rapidly towards Mongrove's. 'Stop thief! Oh! Ah! Thief, thief, *thief!*' His breathing became heavier. He felt dizzy. 'Stop thief!'

Yusharisp, who had been practising how to sit on the couch, gave up and sat on the floor. 'Will there be trouble?' he said.

'I expect so,' said Jherek, hugging himself. 'Yes. *Trouble.*' His eyes were glassy. He stared through the alien.

Yusharisp was touched by what he interpreted as Jherek's nobility. 'Why are you risking so much, then, for a stranger like myself?'

'For love!' whispered Jherek, and another shudder of pleasure ran through him. 'For *love!'*

'You are a great-hearted, skree, creature,' said Yusharisp tenderly. He rose on his hands and knees and looked up at Jherek, his eyes shining. 'Greater, skree, skree, skree, love, as we (roar) say on my planet, hath skree, skree, no man skree, ryof chio lar, oof.' He stopped in embarrassment. 'It must skree, be untranslatable.'

'I'd better change you back into your proper shape before we get to Mongrove's,' said Jherek, his tone becoming businesslike.

CHAPTER EIGHT

A PROMISE FROM MRS AMELIA UNDERWOOD:
A MYSTERY

MONGROVE had been delighted to receive Yusharisp. He had embraced, and almost smothered, the little round space-traveller, beginning immediately to question him on all aspects of his message of doom.

The space-traveller had been pleased by the reception, though he was still under the impression that he was soon to be helped to leave the planet. That was why Jherek Carnelian had made the transaction as quickly as possible and left with his new treasure while Mongrove and Yusharisp were still deep in conversation.

Mrs Amelia Underwood had been stiffened for easy transportation (without her realising that she was to belong to Jherek now) and shipped aboard the locomotive.

Jherek had lost no time in returning to his ranch and there depositing Mrs Underwood in what in ancient times had always been the most important section of the house, the cellar. The cellar was immediately above his bedroom and contained towering transparent tanks of carnelian- and pearl-coloured wine. It was also the prettiest room in the house and he felt Mrs Underwood would be pleased to wake up in such lovely surroundings.

Laying her upon an ottoman bed in the exact centre of the room, Jherek adjusted Mrs Underwood so that she would sleep and awake slowly and naturally the following morning.

He then went to his own bedroom, impatient to prepare himself for when he next encountered her, determined that he should this time make a good impression. Though it was still many hours until morning, he began to make his plans. He intended to wear something ordinary and give up trying to please her by imitation, since she had made no comment on his earlier costume. He made a solid holograph of himself and dressed it in several different styles, making the holograph move about the room wearing the styles until he was satisfied and had selected the one he wanted.

He would wear everything—robes, shoes, hair, eyebrows and lips —in white. He would blend in well with the main décor of the cellar, particularly if he wore only one ring, the rich, red garnet which clung to the third finger of his right hand like a drop of fresh blood.

Jherek wondered if Mrs Underwood would like to change into something different. The grey suit, the white blouse and the straw hat were beginning to look rather crumpled and faded. He decided to construct some clothes for her and take them with him as one of his courting gifts. He had seen enough of the literature of the period to know that the offering of such a gift was a necessary part of the courting ritual and would surely be welcome.

He must think of another gift, too. Something traditional. And music. There must be music playing in the background . . .

When he had made his plans, there were still several hours left and they gave him time to review recent events. He felt a little nervous. My Lady Charlotina was bound to want to repay him for his trick, his theft of her alien. At present he did not want to be interrupted in his courtship and if My Lady Charlotina decided to act at once it could prove inconvenient. He had hoped, of course, to have more time before she discovered his deception. However, it could not be helped. He could only hope now that her vengeance would not take too complicated or prolonged a form.

He lounged in his eight-poster, his body sunk in white cushions, and waited impatiently for morning, refusing to speed up the period of time by a second, for he knew that time-travellers were often thrown out by such things.

He contemplated his situation. He did find Mrs Underwood most attractive. She had a beautiful skin. Her face was lovely. And she seemed quite intelligent, which was pleasant. If she fell in love with him tomorrow (which was pretty inevitable, really) there were all sorts of games they could play—separations, suicides, melancholy walks, bitter-sweet partings and so on. It really depended on her and how her imagination worked with his. The important thing at present was to get the groundwork done.

He slept for a little while, a relaxed, seraphic smile upon his handsome lips.

Then, in the morning, Jherek Carnelian went a-courting.

In his translucent white robes, with his milk-white hair all coiffed and curled, with his white lips smiling, a bunch of little chocolates on long leafy stalks in one hand, a silver 'suitcase' full of clothing in the other, he paused outside the cellar door (of genuine silk stretched on a frame of plaited gold) and stamped twice on the floor in lieu of a knock (how had they managed to knock on the doors? One of many such mysteries). The stamping also had the effect of making the music begin to play. It was a piece by a composer who was a close contemporary of Mrs Underwood's. His name was Charles St Ives, the Cornish Caruso, and his pleasant counter-melodies, through unsophisticated, were probably just the sort of thing that Mrs Underwood would enjoy.

Jherek made the music soft, virtually unhearable at first.

'Mrs Amelia Underwood,' he said. 'Did you hear me knock? Or stamp?'

'I would be grateful if you went away,' said her voice from the other side of the door. 'I know who you are and I can guess why I have been abducted—and to where. If you intend to soften my resolve by inducing madness in me, you shall not have that satisfaction. I will destroy myself first! Monster.'

'My servo brought you breakfast, did it not? I trust it was to your taste.'

Her tone was mocking, a little strained. 'I have never been over-fond of raw beef, sir. Neither is neat whisky my idea of a suitable breakfast drink. At least in my other prison I received the food I rquested.'

'Request, then. I'm sorry, Mrs Amelia Underwood. I was sure I had it right. Perhaps in your region of the world at that time the customs were dissimilar . . . Still, you must tell me——'

'If I am to be a prisoner here, sir,' she said firmly, 'I shall require for breakfast two slices of lightly toasted bread, unsalted butter, Chetwynd's Cheshire Marmalade, café au lait and, occasionally, two medium boiled eggs.'

He made a gesture with his red ring. 'It is done. Programmed.'

Her voice continued:

'For luncheon—well, that will vary. But, since the climate is constantly far too warm, salads of various varieties shall form the basis of the meals. No tomatoes. They are bad for the complexion. I will specify the varieties later. On Sundays—roast beef, mutton, pork or veal. Venison from time to time, in season (though it's inclined to heat the blood, I know) and game when suitable. Mutton cutlets. Stewed ox-cheek and so forth. I'll make you a list. And Yorkshire pudding with the beef, and horseradish sauce, of course, et cetera. Mint sauce with the mutton. Apple sauce with the pork. Peppercorns or sage and onion with the veal, perhaps, though I have certain preferences regarding veal, which I will also list. For dinner . . .'

'Mrs Amelia Underwood!' cried Jherek Carnelian in confusion. 'You shall have every food you wish, any dish which delights you. You shall eat turkeys and turtles, heads, hearts and haunches, gravies and gateaux, fish, fowl and beast shall be created and shall die for the pleasure of your palate! I swear to you that you shall never breakfast off beef and whisky again. And now, Mrs Underwood, may I please come in?'

There was a note of surprise in her voice. 'You are the gaoler, sir. You may do as you please, I am sure!'

The music of Charles St Ives (*Three New Places in England*) grew louder and Jherek stepped backward and then plunged through the silk, catching his foot in a trailing fragment of the stuff and hopping forward without much style, noticing that she was covering her ears and crying:

'Awful! Awful!'

'You are not pleased with the music? It is of your time.'

'It is cacophony.'

'Ah, well.' He snapped his fingers and the music died. He turned and reformed the silk in its frame. Then, with a sweeping bow which rivalled one of Lord Jagged's, he presented himself in all his whiteness to her.

She was dressed in her usual costume, although her hat lay on the neatly made twelve foot long ottoman. She stood framed against a tank of sparkling champagne, her hands folded together under her breasts, her lips pursed. She really was the most beautiful human being apart from himself that Jherek had ever seen. He could have imagined and created nothing better. Little strands of chestnut hair fell over her face. Her grey-green eyes were bright and steady. Her shoulders were straight, her back stiff, her little booted feet together.

'Well, sir?' she said. Her voice was sharp, even cold. 'I see you have abducted me. If you have my body, I guarantee that you shall not have my soul!'

He hardly heard her as he drank in her beauty. He offered her the bunch of chocolates. She did not accept them. 'Drugs,' she said, 'shall not willingly pass my lips.'

'Chocolates,' he explained. He indicated the blue ribbon bound around their stalks. 'See? Blue ribbon.'

'Chocolates.' She peered at them more closely. For a moment she seemed almost amused, but then her face resumed its set, stern expression. She would not take them. At last he was forced to make the chocolates drift over to the ottoman and settle beside her hat. They went well together. He disseminated the suitcase so that the contents tumbled to the floral floor.

'And what is this?'

'Clothes,' he said, 'for you to wear. Aren't they pretty?'

She looked down at the profusion of colours, the variety of materials. They scintillated. Their beauty was undeniable and all the colours suited her. Her lips parted, her cheeks flushed. And then she spurned the clothes with her buttoned boot. 'These are not suitable clothes for a well-bred lady,' she said. 'You may take them away.'

He was disappointed. He was almost *hurt*. 'But——? Away?'

'My own clothes are perfectly satisfactory. I would like the opportunity to wash them, that is all. I have found nowhere in this—this cell—that offers—washing facilities.'

'You are not bored, Mrs Amelia Underwood, with what you are wearing?'

'I am not. As I was saying. Regarding the facilities . . .'

'Well.' He made a gesture with his ring. The clothes at her feet rose into the air, altering shape and colour until they, too, drifted to the ottoman. Beside the chocolates and the straw hat there now lay neatly side by side six identical outfits (complete with straw boaters) each exactly the same as the one she presently wore.

'Thank you.' She seemed just a fraction less cool in manner. 'That is much better.' She frowned. 'I wonder if, after all, you are not . . .'

Grateful that at last he had done something to meet with her approval, he decided to make his announcement. Gathering his robes around him, he went carefully down on one knee upon the curtains of fresh flowers which covered the floor. He placed his two hands upon his heart. He raised his eyes to heaven in a gaze of adoration.

'Mrs Amelia Underwood!'

She took a startled step backward and bumped against a wine tank. It made a faint sloshing.

'I am Jherek Carnelian,' he continued. 'I was born. I love you!'

'Good heavens!'

'I love you more than I love life, dignity, or deities,' he went on. 'I shall love you until the cows come home, until the pigs cease to fly. I, Jherek Carnelian . . .'

'Mr Carnelian!' She was stunned, it seemed, by his devotion. But why should she be stunned? After all everyone was always declaring their love to everyone else in her time! 'Get up, sir, please. I am a respectable woman. I believe that perhaps you are under some misunderstanding considering the position I hold in society. That is, Mr Carnelian—I am a housewife. A housewife from, in fact, Bromley, in Kent, near London. I have no—no *other* occupation, sir.'

'Housewife?'

He looked imploringly at her for an explanation. 'Misunderstanding?'

'I have, I emphasise—no—other—calling.'

He was puzzled. 'You must explain.'

'Mr Carnelian. Earlier I was trying to hint—to touch upon a rather *delicate* matter concerning the, ah, appointments. I cannot find them.'

'Appointments?' Still on one knee he glanced around the cellar, at the great tanks of wine, the jacaranda trees, the sarcophagi, the stuffed alligators and bears, the mangles, the wurlitzer. 'I'm afraid I do not follow . . .'

'Mr Carnelian.' She coughed and lowered her eyes to the floor, murmuring: 'The *bathroom*.'

'But Mrs Amelia Underwood, if you wish to bathe, there are the tanks of wine. Or I can bring aphid's milk, if you prefer.'

Evidently in some embarrassment, but with her manner becoming increasingly insistent, she said: 'I do not wish to bathe, Mr Carnelian. I am referring'—she took a deep breath—'to the water closet.'

Realisation dawned. How obtuse he was. He smiled helpfully. 'I suppose it could be arranged. I can easily fill a closet with water. And we can make love. Oh, in water. Liquid!'

Her lip trembled. She was plainly in distress. Had he again misinterpreted her? Helplessly he stared up at her. 'I love you,' he said.

Her hands leapt to her face. Her shoulders began to heave. 'You must hate me dreadfully.' Her voice was muffled. 'I cannot believe that you do not understand me. As another human being . . . Oh, how you must hate me!'

'No!' He rose with a cry. 'No! I love you. Your every desire will be met by me. Whatever is in my power to do I shall do. It is simply, Mrs Amelia Underwood, that you have not made your request explicit. I do not understand you.' He spread his arms to indicate everything in the room. 'I have carefully reconstructed a whole house in the fashion of your own time. I have done everything, I hope, to suit you. If you will only explain further I will be happy to make what you ask.' He paused. She was lowering her hands from her face and offering him a peculiar, searching look. 'Perhaps a sketch?' he suggested.

She covered her face again. Again her shoulders began to heave.

It took some time before he could discover from her what she wanted. She told him in halting, nervous tones. She blushed deep scarlet.

He laughed delightedly when he understood.

'Such functions have long since been dispensed with by our people. I could restructure your body slightly and you would not need . . .'

'I will not be interfered with!'

'If that is your desire.'

At last he had manufactured her 'bathroom', according to her instructions and put it in one corner of the cellar. Then, at her further request, he boxed it in, adding a touch or two of his own, the vermilion marble, the green baize.

The moment it was finished, she ran inside and closed the door with a slam. He was reminded of a small, nervous animal. He wondered if the box offered her a sense of security which the cellar could not. How long would she remain in the appointment? Forever, like a menagerie specimen which refused to leave its environment? How long *could* she stay there, hidden behind the marble door, refusing to see him? After all, she must fall in love with him soon.

He waited for what seemed to him to be a very long time indeed. Then he weakened and called:

'Mrs Amelia Underwood?'

Her voice came sharply from the other side of the door. 'Mr Carnelian, you have no tact! I may have mistaken your intentions, but I cannot ignore the fact that your manners are abominable!'

'Oh!' He was offended. 'Mrs Amelia Underwood! I am known for my tact. I am famous for it. I was born!'

'So was I, Mr Carnelian. I cannot understand why you keep harping on the fact. I am reminded of some tribesmen we had the misfortune to meet when my father, my mother and myself were in South America. They had some similar phrase . . .'

'They were impolite?'

'It does not matter. Let us say that yours is not the kind of tact an English gentlewoman recognises. One moment.'

There came a gurgling noise and at last she emerged. She looked a little fresher, but she gave him a glance of puzzled displeasure.

Jherek Carnelian had never experienced anything particularly close to misery before, but he was beginning to understand the meaning of the word as he sighed with frustration at his inability to communicate with Mrs Underwood. She was forever misunderstanding his intentions. According to his original calculations they should at this moment be together in the ottoman exchanging kisses and so forth and pledging eternal love to each other. It was all extremely upsetting. He determined to try again.

'I want to make love to you,' he said reasonably. 'Does that mean nothing? I am sure that people constantly made love to each other in your age. I *know* they did. Everything I have studied shows that it was one of the chief obsessions of the time!'

'It is not something we speak about, Mr Carnelian.'

'I want to—to—— What do you say instead?'

'There is, Mr Carnelian, such a thing as the institution of Christian marriage.' Her tone, while softening, also became rather patronising. 'Such love as you speak of is sanctioned by society only if the two people involved are married. I believe you might not be the monster I thought you. You have, in your fashion, behaved in an almost gentlemanly way. I must conclude, therefore, that you are merely misguided. If you wish to learn proper behaviour, then I shall not stand in the way of your learning it. I will do my best to teach you all I can of civilised comportment.'

'Yes?' He brightened. 'This marriage. Shall we do that, then?'

'You wish to marry me?' She gave a tiny, icy laugh.

'Yes.' He began to lower himself to his knees again.

'I am already married,' she explained. 'To Mr Underwood.'

'I have married, too,' he said, unable to interpret the significance of her last statement.

'Then we *cannot* marry, Mr Carnelian.' She laughed again. 'People who are already married must remain married to those people to whom they are—ah—already married. To whom are you married?'

'Oh,' he smiled and shrugged, 'I have been married to many people. To my mother, of course, the Iron Orchid. She was the first, I think, being the closest to hand at the time. And then (second, if not first) Mistress Christia, the Everlasting Concubine. And My Lady Charlotina. And to Werther de Goethe, but that came to very little as I recall. And most recently to Lord Jagged of Canaria, my old friend. And perhaps a hundred others in between.'

'A—a *hundred* others?' She sat down suddenly upon the ottoman. 'A hundred?' She gave him a queer look. 'Do you understand me correctly, Mr Carnelian, when I speak of marriage. Your mother? A male friend? Oh dear!'

'I do not misunderstand you, I am sure. Marriage means making love, does it not.' He paused, trying to think of a more direct phrase. 'Sexual love,' he said.

She leaned back on the ottoman, one delicate hand against her perfect brow. She spoke in a whisper. 'Please, Mr Carnelian! Stop at once. I wish to hear no more. Leave me, I beg you.'

'You do not wish to marry me now?'

'Leave . . .' She pointed a trembling finger at the door. 'Leave . . .'

But he continued patiently: 'I love you, Mrs Amelia Underwood. I brought chocolates—clothes. I made the—the appointments—for you. I declared my everlasting affection. I have stolen for you, cheated and lied for you.' He paused, apologetically. 'I admit I have not yet lost the respect of my friends, but I am trying to think of a way to accomplish that. What else must I do, Mrs Amelia Underwood?'

She rallied a little. She sat upright on the couch and took a very deep breath. 'It is not your fault,' she said, staring fixedly into the middle distance. 'And it is my duty to help. You have asked for my help. I must give it. It would be wicked and unChristian of me to do otherwise. But, frankly, it will be a herculean task. I have lived in India. I have visited Africa. There are few areas of the Empire I have not, in my time, seen. My father was a missionary. He devoted his life to teaching savages the Christian virtues. Therefore . . .'

'Virtue.' Eagerly he shuffled forward on his knees. 'Virtue? That is it. Will you teach me Virtue, Mrs Amelia Underwood?'

She sighed. She had a dazed look on her face now as she looked down at him. It seemed as if she were about to faint. 'How can a Christian refuse? But now you must leave, Mr Carnelian, while I consider the full implications of this situation.'

Again he got to his feet.

'If you say so. I think we're making progress, aren't we? When I have learned virtue—may I then become your lover?'

She made a weary gesture. 'If only you had a bottle of sal volatile. I think it could make all the difference at this moment.'

'Yes? You shall have it. Describe it.'

'No, no. Leave me now. I *must* proceed, I suppose, as if you were not trying to make a joke of my situation, though I have my suspicions. So, until I have complete evidence to the contrary . . . Oh, dear.' She fell back on the ottoman again, having just enough strength to adjust her grey skirt so that its hem did not reveal her ankle.

'I will return later,' he promised. 'To begin my lessons.'

'Later,' she gasped. 'Yes . . .'

He stepped, with a rippling of silk, through the door. He turned and bowed a low, gallant bow.

She stared at him glassily, shaking her head from side to side and running her hand through her chestnut curls.

'My own dear heart,' he murmured.

She felt for the pendant watch lying on her shirt front. She opened the case and looked at the time.

'I shall expect lunch,' she said, 'at exactly one o'clock.'

Almost cheerfully Jherek returned to his bedroom and flung himself upon his cushions.

The courtship was, he had to admit, proving more difficult, more complicated, than he had at first imagined. At least, though, he was soon to learn the secret of that mysterious Virtue. So he had gained something by his acquisition of Mrs Underwood.

His reverie was interrupted by Lord Jagged of Canaria's voice murmuring in his ear:

'May I speak to you, my tasty Jherek, if you are not otherwise engaged? I am below. In your main compartment.'

'Of course.' Jherek got up. 'I'll join you directly.'

Jherek was pleased that Jagged had come. He needed to tell his friend all that had so far taken place between himself and his lady love. Also he wished to seek Lord Jagged's advice on his next moves. Because really, when he thought about it, this was all Lord Jagged's idea . . .

He slipped down into the main room and found Lord Jagged leaning against the bole of the aspidistra, a fruit in his hand. He was nibbling the fruit with a certain clinical interest but no great pleasure. He was dressed in ice blue fog which followed the contours of his body and rose around his pale face in a kind of hood. His limbs were entirely hidden. 'Good morning, Jherek,' he said. He disseminated the fruit. 'And how is your new guest?'

'At first she was unresponsive,' Jherek told him. 'She seemed to think I was unsympathetic. But I think I have broken down her reserve at last. It will not be long before the curtain rises on the main act.'

'She loves you as you love her?'

'She is beginning to love me, I think. She is taking an interest in me, at any rate.'

'So you have not made love?'

'Not yet. There are more rituals involved than you and I guessed. All kinds of things. But it is extremely interesting.'

'You remain in love with her, of course?'

'Oh, of course. Desperately. I'm not one to back out of an affectation just like that, Lord Jagged. You know me better, I hope.'

'I do. I apologise,' murmured the Lord of Canaria, displaying his sharp, golden teeth.

'But, if the story is to assume true *dramatic*, even *tragic*, dimensions, she must, of course, learn to love me. Otherwise the thing becomes a farce, a low comedy, and barely worth pursuing at all!'

'Agreed—oh, *agreed!*' said Jagged. And his smile was strange.

'She is to teach me the customs of her people. She is to prepare me for the main ritual which is called "marriage". Then, doubtless, she will pledge her own love and the thing can begin in earnest.'

'And how long will all this take?'

'Oh, at least a day or two,' said Jherek seriously. 'Perhaps a week.' He remembered another matter. 'And how did My Lady Charlotina take my, um, *crime?*'

'Extremely well.' Lord Jagged strode about the room, leaving little clouds of blue fog behind him. 'She has vowed—let me see—everlasting vengeance upon you. She is even now contemplating the most exquisite form of revenge. The possibilities! You should have been there last night. You would *never* guess some of them. Retribution, my darling Jherek, will strike at the best possible dramatic moment for you, rest assured. And it will be *cruel!* It will be apt. It will be witty!'

Jherek was hardly listening. 'She is very imaginative,' he said.

'Highly.'

'But she plans nothing immediate?'

'I think not.'

'Good. I would rather have time to establish the ritual between Mrs Amelia Underwood and myself before I have to think of My Lady Charlotina's vengeance.'

'I understand.' Lord Jagged lifted his fine head and looked through the wall. 'You're neglecting the scenery a bit, aren't you? Your herds of buffalo haven't moved for quite a while. And your parrots seem to have disappeared altogether. Still, I suppose that is in keeping with someone who is nurturing an obsession.'

'I must, however, extinguish that sunset.' Jherek removed the sunset and the scenery was suddenly flooded with ordinary sunlight, from the sun. It clashed a little, but he didn't mind. 'I'm becoming bored with all the peripheral stuff, I think.'

'And why shouldn't you be? And who is this come to see you?'

An ornithopter, awkward and heavy, came lumbering through the sky, its huge metal wings clashing as they flapped unevenly earthward. It slumped into the corral near Jherek's locomotive. A small figure emerged from the machine.

'Why!' exclaimed Lord Jagged of Canaria. 'It's Brannart Morphail himself. On an errand from My Lady Charlotina, perhaps? The opening sally?'

'I hope not.'

Jherek watched the hunchbacked scientist limp slowly up the steps to the veranda. When he did not use a vehicle, Brannart Morphail insisted on limping everywhere. It was another of his idiosyncrasies. He came through the door and greeted the two friends.

'Good morning, Brannart,' said Lord Jagged, moving forward and clapping the scientist upon his hump. 'What brings you from your laboratories?'

'You remember, I hope, Jherek,' said the chronologist, 'that you agreed to let me see that time-machine today. The new one?'

Jherek had forgotten entirely his hasty—and lying—conversation with Morphail the previous evening.

'The time machine?' he echoed. He tried to remember what he had said. 'Oh, yes.' He decided to make a clean breast of it. 'I'm sorry to say that that was a joke, my dear Morphail. A joke with My Lady Charlotina. Did you not hear about it?'

'No. She seemed pensive when she returned, but I left soon afterward on account of her losing interest in me. What a pity.' Brannart ran his fingers through his streaky, multi-hued beard and hair, but he had accepted the news philosophically enough. 'I had hoped . . .'

'Of course you had, my crusty,' said Lord Jagged, tactfully stepping in. 'Of course, of course, my twisted, tattered love. But Jherek *does* have a time-traveller here.'

'The Piltdown Man?'

'Not exactly. A slightly later specimen. 19th century isn't it, Jherek?' said Lord Jagged. 'A lady.'

'19th century England,' said Jherek, a trifle pedantically, for he was proud of his thorough knowledge of the period.

But Brannart was disappointed. 'Came in a conventional machine, eh? Did she? 19th—20th—21st century or thereabouts. The kind with the big wheels, was it?'

'I suppose so.' Jherek had not thought to ask her. 'I didn't see the machine. Have you seen it, Lord Jagged?'

Lord Jagged shrugged and shook his head.

'When did she arrive?' old Morphail asked.

'Two or three days ago.'

'No time machine has been recorded arriving then,' Morphail said decisively. 'None. We haven't had one through for more than a score of days. And even the last few barely stayed long enough to register on my chronographs. You must find out from your time-traveller, Jherek, what sort of machine she used. It could be important. You could help me, after all! A new kind of machine. Possibly not a machine at all. A mystery, eh?' His eyes were bright.

'If I can help, I'll be pleased to. I feel I have already brought you here on a fool's errand, Brannart.' Jherek assured the scientist. 'I will find out as soon as possible.'

'You are very kind, Jherek.' Brannart Morphail paused. 'Well, I suppose . . .'

'You'll stay to lunch?'

'Ah. I don't lunch, really. And my experiments await. Await. Await.' He waved a thin hand. 'Good-bye for now, my dears.'

They saw him to his ornithopter. It began to clank skyward after a few false starts. Jherek waved to it, but Lord Jagged was looking back at the house and frowning. 'A mystery, eh?' said Jagged.

'A mystery?' Jherek turned.

'A mystery, *too*,' said Lord Jagged. He winked at Jherek.

Wearily, Jherek returned the wink.

CHAPTER NINE

SOMETHING OF AN IDYLL: SOMETHING
OF A TRAGEDY

THE days passed.

My Lady Charlotina took no vengeance.

Lord Jagged of Canaria disappeared upon an errand of his own and no longer visited Jherek.

Mongrove and Yusharisp became enormously good friends and Mongrove was determined to help Yusharisp (who was no engineer) build a new spaceship.

The Iron Orchid became involved with Werther de Goethe and took to wearing nothing but black. She even turned her blood a deep black. They slept together in a big black coffin in a huge tomb of black marble and ebony.

It was, it seemed, to be a season of gloom, of tragedy, of despair. For everyone had by now heard of Jherek's having fallen in love, of his hopeless passion for Mrs Amelia Underwood, of his misery. He had set another fashion into which the world was plunging with even more enthusiasm than it had plunged into Flags.

Ironically, only Jherek Carnelian and Mrs Amelia Underwood were largely untouched by the fashion. They were having a reasonably pleasant time together, as soon as Jherek realised that he was not to consummate his love for a while, and Mrs Underwood understood that he was, in her expression, 'more like a misguided nabob than a consciously evil Caesar'. He did not really know what she was talking about, but he was content to let the subject go since it meant she agreed to share his company during most of her waking hours.

They explored the world in his locomotive. They went for drives in a horse-drawn carriage. They punted on a river which Jherek made for her. She taught him the art of riding the bicycle and they cycled through lovely broadleaf woods which he built according to her instructions, taking packed lunches, a thermos of tea, the occasional bottle of hock. She relaxed (to a large extent) and consented to change her costume from time to time (though remaining faithful to the fashions of her own age). He made her a piano, after some false starts and peculiar mutations, and she sang hymns to him, or sometimes patriotic songs like *Drake's Drum* or *There'll Always Be An England*. At very rare moments she would sing a sentimental song, such as *Come Into The Garden, Maud* or *If Those Lips Could Only Speak*. For a short time he took up the banjo in order to accompany her, but she disapproved of the instrument, it seemed, so he abandoned it.

With a sunshade on her shoulder, with a wide-brimmed Gainsborough hat on her chestnut curls, wearing a frothy summer frock of white cotton trimmed with green lace, she would allow him to take a punt into the air and soar over the world, looking at Mongrove's mountains or the hotsprings of the Duke of Queens, Werther de Goethe's brooding black tomb, Mistress Christia's scented ocean. On the whole they tended to avoid Lake Billy the Kid and the territory of My Lady Charlotina. There was no point, said Mrs Amelia Underwood, in tempting providence.

She described the English Lake District to him and he built her fells and lakes to her specifications, but she was never really happy with the environment.

'You are always inclined to overdo things, Mr Carnelian,' she explained, studying a copy of Lake Thirlmere which stretched for fifty miles in all directions. 'Though you have got the peculiar shifting light right,' she said consolingly. She sighed. 'No. It won't do. I'm sorry.'

And he destroyed it.

This was one of her few disappointments, however, although she had still to get him to understand the meaning of Virtue. She had given up the direct approach and hoped that he would learn by example and through conversations they had concerning various aspects of her own world.

Once, remembering Brannart Morphail's request, he asked her how she had been brought to his world.

'I was abducted,' she told him simply.

'Abducted? By some passing time-traveller who fell in love with you?'

'I never discovered his feelings towards me. I was asleep in my own bed one night when this hooded figure appeared in my room. I tried to scream, but my vocal cords were frozen. He told me to dress. I refused. He told me again, insisting that I wear clothes "typical of my period". I refused and suddenly my clothes were on and I was standing up. He seized me. I fainted. The world spun and then I was in your world, wandering about and trying to find someone in authority, preferably the British Consul. I realise now, of course, that you don't have a British Consul here. That, naturally, is why I am inclined to despair of ever returning to 23 Collins Avenue, Bromley.'

'It sounds very romantic,' said Jherek. 'I can see why you regret leaving.'

'Romantic? Bromley? Well . . .' She let the subject go. She sat with her back straight and her knees together on the plush and ermine seat of his locomotive, peering out at the scenery floating past below. 'However, I should very much like to go back, Mr Carnelian.'

'I fear that's not possible,' he said.

'For technical reasons?' She had never pursued this subject very far before. He had always managed to give her the impression that it was totally impossible rather than simply very difficult to move backward in Time.

'Yes,' he said. 'Technical reasons.'

'Couldn't we visit this scientist you mention? Brannart Morphail? And ask him?'

He didn't want to lose her. His love for her had grown profound (or, at least, he thought it had, not being absolutely sure what 'profound' meant). He shook his head emphatically. Also there were indications that she was beginning to warm towards him. It might be quite soon that she would agree to become his lover. He didn't want her sidetracked.

'Not possible,' he said. 'Particularly since, it seems, you didn't come in a time machine. I've never heard of that before. I thought a machine was always required. Who do you think it was abducted you? Nobody from my age, surely?'

'He wore a hood.'

'Yes.'

'His whole body was hidden by his garments. It might not even have been a man. It could have been a woman. Or a beast from some other planet, such as those kept in your menageries.'

'It really is very strange. Perhaps,' said Jherek fancifully, 'it was a Messenger of Fate—Spanning the Centuries to Bring Two Immortal

Lovers Together Again.' He leaned towards her, taking her hand. 'And here at last——'

She snatched her hand away.

'Mr Carnelian! I thought we had agreed to stop such nonsense!'

He sighed. 'I can hide my feelings from you, Mrs Amelia Underwood, but I cannot banish them altogether. They remain with me night and day.'

She offered him a kind smile. 'It is just infatuation, I am sure, Mr Carnelian. I must admit I would find you quite attractive—in a Bohemian sort of way, of course—if I were not already married to Mr Underwood.'

'But Mr Underwood is a million years away!'

'That makes no difference.'

'It must. He is dead. You are a widow!' He had not wasted his time. He had questioned her closely on such matters. 'And a widow may marry again!' he added cunningly.

'I am only technically a widow, Mr Carnelian, as well you know.' She looked primly up at him as he stalked moodily about the footplate. Once he almost fell from the locomotive so great was his agitation. 'It is my duty to bear in mind always the possibility that I might find a means of returning to my own age.'

'The Morphail Effect,' he said. 'You can't *stay* in the past once you have visited the future. Well, not often. And not for long. I don't know why. Neither does Morphail. Reconcile yourself, Mrs Amelia Underwood, to the knowledge that you must spend eternity here (such as it is). Spend it with me!'

'Mr Carnelian. No more!'

He slouched to the far side of the footplate.

'I agreed to accompany you, to spend my time with you, because I felt it was my duty to try to imbue in you some vestige of a moral education. I shall continue in that attempt. However, if, after a while, it seems to me that there is no hope for you, I shall give up. Then I shall refuse to see you for any reason, whether you keep me prisoner or not!'

He sighed. 'Very well, Mrs Amelia Underwood. But months ago you promised to explain what Virtue was and how I might pursue it. You have still not managed a satisfactory explanation.'

'Nil desperandum,' she said. Her back grew imperceptibly straighter. 'Now . . .'

And she told him the story of Sir Parsifal as the gold, ebony and ruby locomotive puffed across the sky, trailing glorious clouds of blue and silver smoke behind it.

And so the time went by, until both Mrs Amelia Underwood and Jherek Carnelian had become thoroughly used to each other's company. It was almost as if they *were* married (save for one thing— and that did not seem as important as it had, for Jherek was, like all his people, extremely adaptable) and on terms of friendly equality, at that. Even Mrs Amelia Underwood had to admit there were some advantages to her situation.

She had few responsibilities (save her self-appointed responsibility concerning Jherek's moral improvement) and no household duties. She did not need to hold her tongue when she felt like making an astute observation. Jherek certainly did not demand the attention and respect which Mr Underwood had demanded when they had lived together in Bromley. And there had been moments in Mrs Underwood's life in this disgusting and decadent age when she had, for the first time ever, sensed what freedom might mean. Freedom from fear, from care, from the harsher emotions. And Jherek *was* kind. There was no doubting his enormous willingness to please her, his genuine liking for her character as well as her beauty. She wished that things had been different, sometimes, and that she really was a widow. Or, at least, single. Or single and in her own time where she and Jherek might be married in a proper church by a proper priest. When these thoughts came she drove them away firmly.

It was her duty to remember that one day she might have the opportunity of returning to 23 Collins Avenue, Bromley, preferably in the spring of 1896. Preferably on the night of April 4 at three o'clock in the morning (more or less the time she had been abducted) so that then no one might have to wonder what had happened. She was sensible enough to know that no one would believe the truth and that the speculation would be at once more mundane and more lurid than the actuality. That aspect of her return was not, in fact, very attractive.

None-the-less, duty was duty.

It was often hard for her to remember what duty actually was in this—this rotting paradise. It was hard, indeed, to cling to all one's proper moral ideals when there was so little evidence of Satan here— no war, no disease, no sadness (unless it was desired), no death, even. Yet Satan *must* be present. And was, of course, she recalled, in the sexual behaviour of these people. But somehow that did not shock her as much as it had, though it *was* evidence of the most dreadful decadence. Still, no worse, really, than those innocent children, the natives of Pawtow Island in the South Seas, where she had spent two years as her father's assistant after Mother had died. They had had no conception of sin, either.

An intelligent, if conventional, woman, Mrs Amelia Underwood sometimes wondered momentarily if she were doing the right thing in teaching Mr Jherek Carnelian the meaning of virtue.

Not, of course, that he showed any particular alacrity in absorbing her lessons. She did, on occasions, feel tempted to give the whole thing up and merely enjoy herself (within reason) as she might upon a holiday. Perhaps that was what this age represented—a holiday for the human race after millennia of struggle? It *was* a pleasant thought. And Mr Carnelian had been right in one thing—all her friends, her relatives and, naturally, Mr Underwood, her whole society, the British Empire itself (unbelievable though *that* was!) were not only dead a million years, crumbled to dust, they were *forgotten*. Even Mr Carnelian had to piece together what he knew of her world from a few surviving records, references by other, later, ages to the 19th century. And Mr Carnelian was regarded as the planet's greatest specialist in the 19th century. This depressed her. It made her desperate. The desperation made her defiant. The defiance led her to reject certain values which had once seemed to her to be immutable and built solidly into her character. These feelings, luckily, came mainly at night when she was in her own bed and Mr Carnelian was elsewhere.

And sometimes, when she was tempted to leave the sanctuary of her bed, she would sing a hymn until she fell asleep.

Jherek Carnelian would often hear Mrs Amelia Underwood singing at night (he had taken to keeping the same hours as the object of his love) and would wake up in some alarm. The alarm would turn to speculation. He would have liked to have believed that Mrs Underwood was calling to him; some ancient love song like that of the Factory Siren who had once lured men to slavery in the plastic mines. Unfortunately the tunes and the words were more than familiar to him and he associated them with the very antithesis of sexual joy. He would sigh and try, without much success, to go back to sleep as her high, sweet voice sang 'Jesus bids us shine with a pure, clear light . . .' over and over again.

Little by little Jherek's ranch began to change its appearance as

Mrs Underwood made a suggestion here, offered an alternative there, and slowly altered the house until, she assured him, it was almost all that a good Victorian family house should be. Jherek found the rooms rather small and cluttered. He felt uncomfortable in them. He found the food, which she insisted they both eat, heavy and somewhat dull. The little Gothic towers, the wooden balconies, the carved gables, the red bricks offended his aesthetic sensibilities even more than the grandiose creations of the Duke of Queens. One day, while they ate a lunch of cold roast beef, lettuce, cucumber, watercress and boiled potatoes, he put down the cumbersome knife and fork with which, at her request, he had been eating the food and said:

'Mrs Amelia Underwood. I love you. You know that I would do anything for you.'

'Mr Carnelian, we agreed . . .'

He raised his hand. 'But I put it to you, dear lady, that this environment you have had me create has become just a little boring, to say the least. Do you not feel like a change?'

'A—change? But, sir, this is a proper house. You told me yourself that you wished me to live as I had always lived. This is very similar, now, to my own house in Bromley. A little larger, perhaps, and a little better furnished—but I could not resist that. I saw no point in not taking the opportunity to have one or two of the things I might not have had in my—my past life.'

With a deep sigh he contemplated the fireplace with its mantelpiece crammed with little china articles, the absolutely tiny aspidistras and potted palms, the occasional tables, the sideboard, the thick carpets, the dark wallpaper, the gas-mantles, the dull curtains (at the windows), the pictures and the motifs which read, in Mrs Underwood's people's own script VIRTUE IS ITS OWN REWARD or WHAT MEAN THESE STONES?

'A little colour,' he said. 'A little light. A little space.'

'The house is very comfortable,' she insisted.

'Aha.' He returned his attention to the animal flesh and unseasoned vegetables before him (reminiscent, he feared, of Mongrove's table).

'You told me how delighted you were in it all,' she said reasonably. She was puzzled by his despondent manner. Her voice was sympathetic.

'And I was,' he murmured.

'Then?'

'It has gone on,' he said, 'for a long time now, you see. I thought this was merely *one* of the environments you would choose.'

'Oh.' She frowned. 'Hm,' she said. 'Well, we believe in stability, you see, Mr Carnelian. In constancy. In solid, permanent things.' She added apologetically: 'It was our impression that our way of life would endure pretty much unchanged for ever. Improving, of course, but not actually altering very much. We visualised a time when all people would live like us. We believed that everyone wanted to live like us, you see.' She put down her knife and fork. She reached over and touched his shoulder. 'Perhaps we were misguided. We were *evidently* wrong. This is indisputable to me, of course. But I thought you wanted a nice house, that it would help you . . .' She removed her hand from his shoulder and sat back in her mahogany chair. 'I do feel just a little guilty, I must say. I did not consider that your feelings might be less than gratified by all this . . .' She waved her hands about to indicate the room and its furnishings. 'Oh, dear.'

He rallied. He smiled. He got up. 'No, no. If this is what you want, then it is what *I* want, of course. It will take a bit of getting used to, but . . .' He was at a loss for words.

'You are unhappy, Mr Carnelian,' she said softly. 'I do not believe I have ever seen you unhappy before.'

'I have never *been* unhappy before,' he said. 'It is an experience. I must learn to relish it, as Mongrove relishes his misery. Though Mongrove's misery seems to have rather more flair than mine. Well, this is what I desired. This is what is doubtless involved in love—and Virtue, too, perhaps.'

'If you wish to send me back to Mr Mongrove . . .' she began nobly.

'No! Oh, no! I love you too much.'

This time she made no verbal objection to his declaration. 'Well,' she said determinedly, 'we must make an effort to cheer you up. Come—' She stretched out her hand. Jherek took her hand. He thrilled. He wondered.

She led him into the parlour where the piano was. 'Perhaps some jolly hymn?' she suggested. 'What about "All Things Bright and Beautiful"?' She smoothed her skirt under her as she sat down on the stool. 'Do you know the words now?'

He could not get the words out of his mind. He had heard them too often, by night as well as by day. Dumbly he nodded.

She struck a few introductory chords on the piano and began

to sing. He tried to join in, but the words would not come out. His throat felt both dry and tight. Amazed, he put his hand to his neck. Her own voice petered out and she stopped playing, swinging round on the stool to look up at him. 'What about a walk?' she said.

He cleared his throat. He tried to smile. 'A walk?'

'A good brisk walk, Mr Carnelian, often has a palliative effect.'

'All right.'

'I'll get my hat.'

A few moments later she joined him outside the house. The grounds of the house were not very large either, now. The prairie, the buffalo, the cavalrymen and the parrots had been replaced by neat privet hedges (some clipped into ornamental shapes), shrubs and rock gardens. The most colour was supplied by the rose garden which had several different varieties, including one which she had allowed him to invent for her, the Mrs Amelia Underwood, which was a bluish green.

She closed the front door and put her arm in his. 'Where shall we go?' she said.

Again the touch of her hand produced the thrill and the thrill was, astonishingly, translated into a feeling of utter misery.

'Wherever you think,' he said.

They went up the crazy-paving path to the garden gate, out of the gate and along the little white road in which stood several gas lamps. The road led up between two low, green hills. 'We'll go this way,' she said.

He could smell her. She was warm. He looked bleakly at her lovely face, her glowing hair, her pretty summer frock, her neat, well-proportioned figure. He turned his head away with a stifled sob.

'Oh, come along now, Mr Carnelian. You'll soon feel better once you've some of this good, fresh air in your lungs.' Passively he allowed her to lead him up the hill until they walked between lines of tall cypresses which fringed fields in which cows and sheep grazed, tended by mechanical cowherds and shepherds who could not, even close to, be told from real people.

'I must say,' she told him, 'this landscape is as much a work of art as any of Reynolds' pictures. I could almost believe I was in my own, dear Kent countryside.'

The compliment did not relieve his gloom.

They crossed a little crooked bridge over a tinkling stream. They entered a cool, green wood of oaks and elms. There were even rooks nesting in the elms and red squirrels running along the boughs of the oaks.

But Jherek's feet dragged. His step became slower and slower and at last she stopped and looked closely up into his face, her own face full of tenderness.

And, in silence, he took her awkwardly in his arms. She did not resist him. Slowly the depression began to lift as their faces drew closer together. Gradually his spirits rose until, at the very moment their lips touched, he knew an ecstasy such as he had never known before.

'My dear,' said Mrs Amelia Underwood. She was trembling as she pressed her precious form against him and put her arms around him. 'My own, dear, Jherek . . .'

And then she vanished.

She was gone. He was alone.

He gave a great scream of pain. He whirled, looking everywhere for some sign of her. 'Mrs Amelia Underwood! Mrs Amelia Underwood!'

But all there was of her was the wood, with its oaks and its elms, its rocks and its squirrels.

He rose into the air and sped back to the little house, his coat-tails flapping, his hat flying from his head.

He ran through the overfurnished rooms. He called to her but she did not reply. He knew that she would not. Everything she had had him create for her—the tables, the sofas, the chairs, the beds, the cabinets, the knick-knacks, seemed to mock him in his grief and thus increase the pain.

And at last he collapsed upon the grass of the rose garden and, holding a rose of a peculiar bluish-green, he wept, for he knew very well what had happened.

Lord Jagged? Where was he? Lord Jagged had told Jherek that it *would* happen like this.

But Jherek had changed. He could no longer appreciate the splendid irony of the joke. For everyone but Jherek would see it as a joke and a clever one.

My Lady Charlotina had claimed her vengeance.

CHAPTER TEN

THE GRANTING OF HER HEART'S DESIRE

My Lady Charlotina would have hidden Mrs Amelia Underwood very well. As he recovered a little of his composure Jherek began to wonder how he might rescue his love. There would be no point in going to My Lady Charlotina's (his first impulse) and simply demanding the return of Mrs Underwood. My Lady Charlotina would only laugh at him the more. No, he must visit Lord Jagged of Canaria and seek his advice. He wondered, now, why Lord Jagged had not come to visit him since he had taken up with Mrs Amelia Underwood. Perhaps Jagged had stayed away out of a rather over-developed sense of tact?

With a heavy heart Jherek Carnelian went to the outbuilding where, at Mrs Underwood's suggestion he had stored his locomotive.

The door of the outbuilding was opened with a key, but he could not find the key. Mrs Underwood had always kept it.

He was reluctant to disseminate the outbuilding now (she had been a stickler about observing certain proprieties of her own day and the business of keys and locks was one of the chief ones, it seemed), for all that it was frightfully ugly. But, with her disappearance, everything of Mrs Underwood's had become sacred to him. If he never found her again this little Gothic house would stand in the same spot forever.

At length, however, he was forced to disseminate the door, order the locomotive out, and remake the door behind him. Then he set off.

As he flew towards Lord Jagged's the thought kept recurring to him that My Lady Charlotina would have seen nothing particularly wrong in disseminating Mrs Amelia Underwood completely and irrevocably. It was unlikely that My Lady Charlotina would have gone that far—but it *was* possible. In that case Mrs Underwood might be gone forever. She could not be resurrected if every single atom of her being had been broken down and spread across the face of the Earth. Jherek kept this sort of thought back as best he could.

If he brooded on it there was every chance, he feared, of his falling into a depressive trance from which he would never wake.

The locomotive at last reached Lord Jagged's castle—all bright yellow, in the shape of an ornamental bird cage and a modest seventy-five feet tall—and began to circle while Jherek sent a message to his friend.

'Lord Jagged? Can you receive a visitor? It is I, Jherek Carnelian, and my business is of the gravest importance.'

There was no reply. The locomotive circled lower. There were various 'boxes' suspended on antigravity beams in the birdcage. Each box was a room used by Lord Jagged. He might be in any one of them. But, no matter which room he occupied, he would be bound to hear Jherek's request.

'Lord Jagged?'

It was plain that Lord Jagged was not at home. There was a sense of desertion about his castle as if it had not been used for several months. Had something happened to the Lord of Canaria?

Had My Lady Charlotina taken vengeance on him, too, for his part in the theft of the alien?

Oh, this was savage!

Jherek turned his locomotive towards the North and Werther de Goethe's tomb, expecting to find that his mother, the Iron Orchid, had also vanished.

But Werther's tomb—a vast statue of himself lying serenely dead with a gigantic Angel of Death hovering over his body and several sorrowing women kneeling beside him—was still occupied by the black pair. They were, in fact, on the roof near the feet of the reclining statue but Jherek did not see them at first, for both they and the statue were completely black.

'Jherek, my sorrow!' His mother sounded almost animated. Werther merely glowered and gnawed his fingernails in the background as the locomotive landed on the flat parapet, bringing a startling dash of colour to the scene. 'Jherek, what ill tidings bring you here?' His mother produced a black handkerchief and wiped black tears from her black cheeks.

'Ill tidings, indeed,' he said. He felt offended by what at the present moment seemed to him to be a mockery of his real anguish. 'Mrs Amelia Underwood has been abducted—perhaps destroyed—and My Lady Charlotina is almost certainly the cause of it.'

'Her *vengeance*, of course!' breathed the Iron Orchid, her black eyes widening and a certain kind of amusement glinting in them. 'Oh! Oh! Woe! Thus is great Jherek brought low! Thus is the House of Carnelian ruined! Oi moi! Oi moi!' And she added, conversationally, 'What do you think of that last touch?'

'This is serious, mother, who brought me precious life . . .'

'Only so that you might suffer its torments! I know! I know! Oh, woe!'

'Mother!' Jherek was screaming. 'What shall I do?'

'What *can* you do?' Werther de Goethe broke in. 'You are doomed, Jherek. You are damned! Fate has singled you out, as it has singled me out, for an eternity of anguish.' He uttered his bitter laugh. 'Accept this dreadful knowledge. There is no solution. No escape. You were granted a few short moments of bliss so that you might suffer all the more exquisitely when the object of your bliss was snatched from you.'

'You know what happened?' Jherek asked suspiciously.

Werther looked embarrassed. 'Well, My Lady Charlotina did take me into her confidence a week or two ago . . .'

'Devil!' cried Jherek. 'You did not try to warn me?'

'Of the inevitable? What good would it have done? And,' said Werther sardonically, 'we all know how prophets are treated these days! People do not like to hear the truth!'

'Wretch!' Jherek turned to confront the Iron Orchid. 'And you, mother, did you know what Charlotina planned?'

'Not exactly, my misery. She merely said something about granting Mrs Underwood her heart's desire.'

'And what is that? What can it be but a life with me?'

'She did not explain.' The Iron Orchid dabbed at her eyes. 'She feared, no doubt, that I would betray her plan to you. After all, we are of the same fickle flesh, my egg.'

Jherek said grimly: 'I see there is nothing for me to do but confront My Lady Charlotina herself.'

'Is this not what you wanted?' said Werther, sitting on a ledge above their heads, leaning his black back against his statue's marble knee and moodily swinging his legs. 'Did you not court disaster when you courted Mrs Underwood? I seem to recall some plan . . .'

'Be silent! I love Mrs Underwood more than I love myself!'

'Jherek,' said his mother reasonably, 'you can take these things too far, you know.'

'There it is! I am thoroughly in love. I am totally in love. My passion rules me. It is no longer a game!'

'No longer a game!' Even Werther de Goethe sounded shocked. 'Farewell, black, black betrayers. Traitors in jet—farewell!'

And Jherek swept back to his locomotive, pulled the whistle and hurled his aircar high into the dark and cheerless sky.

'Do not struggle against your destiny, Jherek!' he heard Werther cry. 'Shake not your fist against uncompromising Fate! Plead not for mercy from the Norns, for they are deaf and blind!'

Jherek did not reply. Instead he let a great sob escape his lips and he murmured her name and the sound of her name brought all the aching anguish back to his soul so that at last he was silent.

And he came to Lake Billy the Kid, all serene and dancing in the sunlight, and he had a mind to destroy the Lake and Under-the-Lake and My Lady Charlotina and her menagerie and her caverns—to destroy the whole globe if need be. But he contained his rage, for Mrs Amelia Underwood might even now be a prisoner in one of those caverns.

He left his locomotive drifting a few inches above the surface of the lake and he went through the Gateway in the Water and came to the cave with the walls of gold and the roof and floor of mirrored silver and My Lady Charlotina was waiting for him, knowing that he would come.

'I knew that you would come, my victim,' she purred.

She was dressed in a gown of lily-coloured stuff through which her soft, pink body might be observed. And her pale hair was piled upon her head and secured by a coronet of platinum and pearls. And her face was serene and stern and proud and her eyes were narrowed and pleased and she smiled at him. She smiled at him. And she lay upon a couch covered in white samite over which white roses had been strewn. All the roses were white save one and that one she fingered. It was a rose of a peculiar bluish-green colour. Even as he approached her she opened her mouth and, with sharp, ivory teeth, plucked a petal from the rose and tore that petal into tiny pieces which flecked her red lips and her chin and fell upon her bodice.

'I knew you would come.'

He stretched out his arms and his hands became claws and he walked on stiff legs with his eyes on her long throat and would have seized her had not a force barrier stopped him, a force barrier of her own recipe which he could not neutralise.

He paused then.

'You are without wit, or charm, or beauty, or grace,' he said sharply.

She was taken aback. 'Jherek! Isn't that a little strong?'

'I mean it!'

'Jherek! Your humour! Where is it? Where? I thought you'd be amused at this turn of events. I planned it so carefully.' She had the air of a disappointed hostess, of someone who had given a party like that of the Duke of Queens (which nobody, of course, had forgotten or would forget until the Duke of Queens, who was still upset by it, managed to conceive some really out of the ordinary entertainment).

'Yes! And all knew of the plan, save myself and Mrs Amelia Underwood.'

'But that, naturally, was an important part of the jest!'

'My Lady Charlotina, you have gone too far! Where is Mrs Amelia Underwood? Return her to me at once!'

'I shall not!'

'And, for that matter, what have you done with Lord Jagged of Canaria? He is not in his castle.'

'I know nothing of Lord Jagged. I haven't seen him for months. Jherek! What is the matter with you? I was expecting some counter-jest. Is this it? If so, it is a poor return for mine . . .'

'The Iron Orchid said that you granted Mrs Underwood her heart's desire. What did you mean by that?'

'Jherek! You're becoming dull. This is extraordinary. Come and make love to me, Jherek, if nothing else!'

'I loathe you.'

'Loathe? How interesting! Come and make——'

'What did you mean?'

'What I said. I gave her the thing she desired most.'

'How could you know what she desired most?'

'Well, I took the liberty of sending a little eavesdropper, a mechanical flea, to listen to some of your conversations. It soon became evident what she wanted most. And so I waited for the right moment, today—and then I did it!'

'Did what? Did what?'

'Jherek you have lost all your wit. Can't you guess?'

He frowned. 'Death? She did at one point say that she would prefer death to . . .'

'No, no!'

'Then what?'

'Oh, what a bore you have become! Let me make love to you and then . . .'

'Jealousy! Now I understand. You love me yourself. You have destroyed Mrs Underwood because you think that then I will love you. Well, madam, let me tell you——'

'Jealousy? Destroyed? Love? Jherek, you have thrown yourself thoroughly into your part, I can see. You are most convincing. But, I fear, something is missing—some hint of irony which would give the role a little more substance.'

'You must tell me, My Lady Charlotina, what you have done with Mrs Amelia Underwood.'

She yawned.

'Tell me!'

'Mad, darling Jherek, I granted her . . .'

'What did you do?'

'Oh, very well! Brannart!'

'Brannart?'

The hunchbacked scientist limped from one of the tunnel mouths and began to cross the mirrored floor, looking down appreciatively at his appearance.

'What has Brannart Morphail to do with this?' Jherek demanded.

'I had to employ his help. And he was eager to experiment.'

'Experiment?' said Jherek in a horrible whisper.

'Hello, Jherek. Well, she'll be there now. I only hope it's successful. If so, then it will open up new roads of inquiry for me. I am still interested in the fact that she did not come here in a time machine . . .'

'What have you done, Brannart?'

'What? Well, I sent her back to her own time, of course. In one of the machines in my collection. If all went well she should be there by now. April 4, 1896, 3 a.m. Bromley, Kent, England. Temporal co-ordinates should offer no real trouble, but there might be a slight variance on the spatial. So unless something happened on the way back—you know, a chronostorm or something—she will . . .'

'You mean—you sent her back to . . . Oh!' Jherek sank to his knees in despair.

'Her heart's desire,' said My Lady Charlotina. 'Now do you appreciate the succulent irony of it, my tragic Jherek? See how I have produced your reversal? Isn't it a charming revenge? Surely you are amused?'

Jherek did his best to rally himself. Shaking, he raised himself to his feet and he looked past the smiling Lady Charlotina at Brannart Morphail who, as usual, had missed all the nuances.

'Brannart. You must send me there, too. I must follow her. She loves me. She was on the point of declaring that love . . .'

'I know! I know!' My Lady Charlotina clapped her hands.

'Of declaring that love, when she was snatched from me. I must pursue her—across a million years if need be—and bring her back. You must help me, Brannart.'

'Ah!' My Lady Charlotina giggled with delight. 'Now I understand you, Jherek. How daring! How clever! Of course—it has to be! Brannart, you must help him.'

'But the Morphail Effect . . .' Brannart Morphail stretched his hands imploringly out to her. 'It is highly unlikely that the past will accept Mrs Underwood back. It might propel her into her own near future—in fact that's the most likely thing—but it will send Jherek anywhere, back here, further forward, to oblivion possibly. Visitors from the future cannot exist in the past. The traffic is, effectively, one-way. That is the Morphail Effect.'

'You will do as I ask, Brannart,' said Jherek. 'You will send me back to 1896.'

'You may have only a few seconds in that time—I cannot guarantee how long—before it—it spits you out.' Brannart Morphail spoke slowly, as if to an idiot. 'To make the attempt is dangerous enough. You could be destroyed in any one of a dozen different ways, Jherek. Take my advice . . .'

'You will do as he asks, Brannart,' said My Lady Charlotina, tossing aside the rose of a peculiar bluish-green. 'Can you not appreciate a properly realised drama when it is presented to you? What else can Jherek do? It is inevitable.'

Again Brannart objected, growling to himself. But My Lady Charlotina drifted over to him and whispered something in his ear and the growling ceased and he nodded. 'I will do what you want, Jherek, though it is, in all senses, a waste of time.'

CHAPTER ELEVEN

THE QUEST FOR BROMLEY

THE time machine was a sphere full of milky fluid in which the traveller floated enclosed in a rubber suit, breathing through a mask attached to a hose leading into the wall of the machine.

Jherek Carnelian looked at it in some distaste. It was rather small, rather battered. There were what looked like scorch marks on its metallic sides.

'Where did it come from, Brannart?' He stretched his rubber-swathed limbs.

'Oh, it could be from almost anywhere. In deciphering the internal dating system I came to the conclusion that it's from a period about two thousand years before the period you want to visit. That's why I chose it for you. It seemed that it might slightly improve your chances.' Brannart Morphail pottered about his laboratory, which was crammed with instruments and machinery, most of them in various stages of disrepair, from many different ages. Most of the least sophisticated looking instruments were the inventions of Brannart Morphail himself.

'Is it safe?' Gingerly Jherek touched the pitted metal of the sphere. Some cracks appeared to have been welded over. It had done a lot of service, that time machine.

'Safe? What time machine is safe? It's as safe as any other.' Brannart waved a dismissive hand. 'It is you, Jherek, who want to travel in it. I have tried to dissuade you from pursuing this folly further.'

'Brannart, you have no imagination. No sense of drama, Brannart,' chided My Lady Charlotina, her eyes twinkling as she lounged on her couch in a corner of the laboratory.

Taking a deep breath, Jherek clambered into the machine and adjusted his breathing apparatus before lowering himself into the fluid.

'You are a *martyr*, Jherek Carnelian!' sighed My Lady Charlotina. 'You may *perish* in the service of temporal exploration. You will be remembered as a Hero, should you die—crucified, tempestuous time-traveller, Casanova of Chrononauts, upon the Cross of Time!' Her couch sped forward and she reached out to press in his right hand a translation pill and, into his left, a crushed rose of a peculiar, bluish-green.

'I intend to save her, My Lady Charlotina, to bring her back.' His voice came out as a somewhat muffled squeak.

'Of course you do! And you are a splendid saviour, Jherek!'

'Thank you.' He still maintained a cool attitude towards her. She seemed to have forgotten that it was because of her that he was forced into this dangerous action.

Her couch fell back. She waved a green handkerchief. 'Speed through the hours, my Horos! Through the days and the months! The centuries and the millennia, most dedicated of lovers—as Hitler sped to Eva. As Oscar sped to Bosie! On! On! Oh, I am *moved*. I am entranced. I am *faint* with rapture!'

Jherek scowled at her, but he took her gifts with him as he slipped deeper into the sphere and felt the airlock close over his head. He floated, uncomfortably weightless, and readied himself for his plunge into the timestream.

Through the fluid he could see the instruments, cryptographic, unconventional, seeming to swim, as he swam, in the fluid. They made no sound, there was no movement on their faces.

Then one of the dials flickered. A series of green and red figures came and went. Jherek's stomach grew tight.

He felt his body shift. Then it was still again. It seemed that the machine had rolled over.

He could hear his breath hissing in the tube. The machine was so uncomfortable, the rubber suit so restricting, that he was almost on the point of suggesting they try a different machine.

Then the same dial flickered again. Green and red. Then two more dials came to life. Blue and yellow. A white light flashed rapidly. The speed of the flashing grew faster and faster.

He heard a gurgling noise. A thump. The liquid in which he floated became darker and darker.

He felt pain (he had never really felt physical pain before).

He screamed, but his voice was muffled.

He was on his way.

He fainted.

He woke up. He was being jolted horribly. The sphere seemed to have cracked. The fluid was rushing out of the crack and as a result his body was being bumped from side to side as the sphere rolled along. He opened his eyes. He closed them. He wailed.

Air hissed as the tube was wrenched from his face. The plastic lining of the machine began to sink until Jherek lay with his back against the metal of the wall, realising that the sphere had stopped rolling. He groaned. He was bruised everywhere. Still, he consoled himself, he *was* suffering now. No one could doubt that.

He looked at the jagged crack in the sphere. He would have to find another time machine, wherever he was, for this one had failed to take the strain of the trip. If he was in 1896 and could find Mrs Amelia Underwood (assuming that she, herself, had arrived back safely) he would have to approach an inventor and borrow a machine. Still, that was the slightest difficulty he would encounter, he was sure.

He tried to move his body and yelped as what had been a relatively dull pain turned, for a moment, into throbbing agony. The pain slowly died. He shivered as he felt the cold air blowing through the time machine's ruptured wall. It seemed to be dark beyond the crack.

He got up, wincing, and stripped off the suit. Underneath was his crumpled Victorian coat and trousers, in a delicate scarlet and purple. He checked that his power rings were still on his fingers and was satisfied. There was the ruby, there the emerald and there the diamond. The air, while cold, also smelled very strange, very thick. He coughed.

He edged his way to the crack and stepped through into the darkness. It was extremely misty. The machine seemed to have landed on some hard, man-made surface, on the edge of a stretch of water. A flight of stone steps led up through the mist and it was probable that the machine had bumped down these before it shattered. High above he could see a dim light, a yellow light, flickering.

He shivered.

This was not what he had expected. If he were in Dawn Age London, then the whole city was deserted! He had imagined it to be packed with people—with millions of people, for this was also the age of the Multitude Cultures.

He decided to make for the light. He stumbled towards the steps. He touched his face and felt the dampness clinging to it. Then he realised what it was he was experiencing and he gave an involuntary sigh of delight.

'Fog . . .'

It was fog.

Rather more cheerfully he felt his way up the steps and eventually struck his shoulder against a metal column. On the top of the column glowed a gas-lamp very similar to those Mrs Amelia Underwood had asked him to make for her. He patted the lamp. He was in the right period at least. Brannart Morphail had been unduly pessimistic.

But was it the right place. Was this Bromley? He looked back through the fog at the wide stretch of murky water. Mrs Underwood had spoken much of Bromley, but she had never mentioned a large river. Still, it could be London, which was near Bromley, and, if so, that river was the Thames. Something hooted from the depths of the fog. He heard a thin, distant shout. Then there was silence again.

He found himself in a narrow alley-way with an uneven, cobbled surface. There were sheets of paper pasted on the dark, brick walls on both sides of the alley. Jherek saw that the paper was covered in graphics and writing but, of course, he could not read anything. Even the translation pills, which worked their subtle engineering upon the brain cells, could not teach him to decipher a written language. He realised that he was still holding the pill My Lady Charlotina had given him. He would wait until he met someone before swallowing it. In his other hand was the crushed rose; all, for the present, that he had left of Mrs Amelia Underwood.

The alley opened onto a street and here the fog was a little lighter. He could see a few yards in both directions and there were several more lamps whose yellow light tried to penetrate the fog.

But still the place seemed deserted as he followed the street, looking with fascination at house after crumbling house as he passed. A few of the houses did have lights shining from behind the blinds at their windows. Once or twice he heard a muffled voice. For some reason, then, the population was staying inside. Doubtless he would find an answer to this mystery in time.

The next street he reached was wider still and here were taller houses (though in the same decrepit state) with their lower windows displaying a variety of objets d'art—here sewing machines, mangles, frying pans—there beds and chairs, tools and clothing. He paused every minute to glance in at these windows. The owners were right to display their treasures so proudly. And what a profusion! Admittedly some of the objects were a little smaller, a little darker, than he had imagined and many, of course, he could not recognise at all. However, when he and Mrs Underwood returned, he would be able to make her considerably more artefacts to please her and remind her of home.

Now he could see a more intense light ahead. And he saw human figures there, heard voices. He struck off across the street and at that moment his ears were filled by a peculiar clacking noise, a rattling noise. He heard a shout. He looked to his left and saw a black beast emerging from the fog. Its eyes rolled, its nostrils flared.

'A horse!' he cried. 'It is a horse!'

He had often made his own, of course, but it was not the same as seeing the original.

Again the shout.

He shouted back, cheering and waving his arms.

The horse was drawing something behind it—a tall black carriage on top of which perched a man with a whip. It was the man who was shouting.

The horse stood up on its hind legs as Jherek waved. It seemed to him that the horse was waving back to him. Strange to be greeted by a beast upon one's first arrival in a century.

Then Jherek felt something strike him on the head and he fell down and to one side as the horse and carriage clattered past and disappeared into the fog.

Jherek tried to get up, but he felt faint again. He groaned. There were people running towards him now, from the direction of the bright light. Soon, as he raised himself to his hands and knees, he saw about a dozen men and women all, like himself, dressed in period, standing in a circle around him. Their faces were heavy and serious. None of them spoke at first.

'What——?' He realised that they would not understand him. 'I apologise. If you wait one moment . . .'

Then they were all babbling at once. He raised the translation pill to his lips and swallowed it.

'Foreigner o' some kind. A Russian, most likely, round 'ere. Off one o' ther boats . . .' he heard a man say.

'Have you any idea what happened to me just then?' Jherek asked him.

The man looked astonished and pushed his battered bowler hat onto the back of his head. 'I coulda swore you wos a foreigner!'

'You wos knocked darn by an 'ansom, that's wot 'appened to you, me ole gonoph,' said another man in a tone of great satisfaction. This man wore a large cloth cap shading his eyes. He put his hands into the pockets of his trousers and continued sagely: ''Cause you waved at the 'orse an' made it rear up, didn't you?'

'Aha! And one of its hoofs struck my head, eh?'

'Yus!' said the first man in a tone of congratulation, as if Jherek had just passed a difficult test.

One of the women helped Jherek to get to his feet. She seemed a bit wrinkled and she smelt very strongly of something Jherek could not identify. Her face was covered in a variety of paints and powders.

She leered at him.

Politely, Jherek leered back.

'Thank you,' he said.

'That's all right, lovey,' said the lady. ''Ad one too many meself, I reckon.' She laughed a harsh, cackling laugh and addressed the gathering in general. ''Aven't we all, at two o'clock in the morning? I can tell you're a toff,' she told him, looking him up and down. 'Bin to a party, 'ave you? Or maybe you're an artiste—a performer, eh?' She twitched her hips and made her long skirt swing.

'I'm sorry . . .' said Jherek. 'I don't . . .'

'There, there,' she said, planting a wet kiss on his moist and dirty face. 'Wanna warm bed fer the night, do yer?' She snuggled her body against him, adding in a murmur for his ears alone. 'It won't cost yer much. I like the looks o' you.'

'You wish to make love to me?' he said, realisation dawning. 'I'm flattered. You are very wrinkled. It would be interesting. Unfortunately, however, I am——'

'Cheek!' She dropped her arm from his. 'Bleedin' cheek! Nasty drunken bastard!' She flounced off while all the others jeered after her.

'I offended her, I think,' said Jherek. 'I didn't mean to.'

'Somefink of an achievement, that,' said a younger man wearing a yellow jacket, brown trousers and a brown, curly-brimmed bowler. He had a thin, lively face. He winked at Jherek. 'Elsie *is* gettin' on a bit.'

The concept of age had never really struck Jherek before, though he knew it was a feature of this sort of period. Now, as he looked around him at the people and saw that they were in different stages of decay, he realised what it meant. They had not deliberately moulded their features in this way. They had no choice.

'How interesting,' he said to himself.

'Well, 'ave a *good* look,' said one of the men. 'Be my guest!'

Understanding that he was about to offend another one, Jherek quickly apologised. Then he pointed to the source of the light. 'I was on my way over there. What is it?'

'That's the coffee-stall,' said the young man in the yellow coat. 'The very hub of Whitechapel, that is. As Piccadilly is to the Empire, so Charley's coffee-stall is to the East End. You'd better 'ave a cup while you're at it. Charley's coffee'll kill or cure you, that's for certain!'

The young man led Jherek to a square van which was open on one side. From the opening a canvas awning extended for several feet and under this awning the customers were now reassembling. Inside the van were several large metal containers (evidently hot), a lot of white china cups and plates and a variety of different objects which were probably food of some kind. A big man with whiskers and the reddest face Jherek had ever seen stood in the van, his shirt-sleeves rolled up, a striped apron over his chest, and served the other people with cups of liquid which he drew from the metal containers.

'I'll pay for this one,' said the young man generously.

'Pay?' said Jherek as he watched the young man hand some small brown discs to the bewhiskered one who served out the cups and plates. In exchange the young man received two china cups. He handed one to Jherek who gasped as the heat was absorbed by his fingers. Gingerly, he sipped the stuff. It was bitter and sweet at the same time. He quite liked it.

The young man was looking Jherek over. 'You speak good English,' he said.

'Thanks,' said Jherek, 'though really it's no reflection on my talents. A translation pill, you know.'

'Do what?' said the young man. But he didn't pursue the matter. His mind seemed to be on other things as he sipped his coffee and glanced absently around him. 'Very good,' he said. 'I'd have taken you for an English gent, straight. If it wasn't for the clothes, o' course—and that language you was speaking just after you was knocked down. Come off a ship, have you?' His eyes narrowed as he spoke.

'In a manner of speaking,' said Jherek. There was no point in mentioning the time machine at this stage. The helpful young man might want to take him to an inventor right away and get him a new one. His main interest at present was in finding Mrs Amelia Underwood. 'Is this 1896?' he asked.

'What, the year? Yes, of course. April Four, 1896. D'you reckon the dates different, then, where you come from?'

Jherek smiled. 'More or less.'

The other people were beginning to drift away, calling good night to one another as they left.

'Night night, Snoozer,' called a woman to the young man.

'Night, Meggo.'

'You're called Snoozer?' said Jherek.

'Right. Nickname.' Snoozer lifted the index finger of his right hand and laid it alongside his nose. He winked. 'What's your monnicker, mate?'

'My name? Jherek Carnelian.'

'I'll call you Jerry, eh? All right.'

'Certainly. And I'll call you Snoozer.'

'Well, about that——' Snoozer put down his empty cup on the counter. 'Maybe you could call me Mr Vine—which is by way of being my real name, see? I wouldn't mind, in the normal course of things, but where we're going "Mr Vine" would sound more respectable, see?'

'Mr Vine it is. Tell me, Mr Vine, is Bromley hereabouts?'

'Bromley in Kent?' Snoozer laughed. 'It depends what you mean. You can get to it fast enough on the train. Less than half-an-hour from Victoria Station—or is it Waterloo? Why, you got some relative there, have you?'

'My—um—betrothed.'

'Young lady, eh? English, is she?'

'I believe so.'

'Good for you. Well, I'll help you get to Bromley, Jerry. Not tonight, o' course, because it's too late. You got somewhere to stay, 'ave you?'

'I hadn't considered it.'

'Ah, well that's all right. How'd you like to sleep in a nice hotel bed tonight—no charge at all? A comfortable bed in a posh West End hotel. At my expense.'

'You're very kind, Mr Vine.' Really, thought Jherek, the people of this age were extremely friendly. 'I *am* rather cold and I am extremely battered.' He laughed.

'Yes, your clothes could do with a bit of a cleaning, eh?' Snoozer Vine fingered his chin. 'Well, I think I can help you there, too. Fix you up with a fresh suit of clothes and everything. And you'll need some luggage. Have you got any luggage?'

'Well, no. I——'

'Don't say another word. Luggage will be supplied. Supplied, Jerry, my friend, courtesy of Snoozer's suitcase emporium. What was your last name again?'

'Carnelian.'

'Carnell. I'll call you Carnell, if you don't mind.'

'By all means, Mr Vine.'

Snoozer Vine uttered a wild and cheerful laugh. 'I can see we're going to get on like old friends, Lord Carnell.'

'Lord?'

'*My* nickname for *you*, see? All right?'

'If it pleases you.'

'Good. Good. What a card you are, Jerry! I think our association's going to be very profitable indeed.'

'Profitable?'

He slapped Jherek heartily on the back. 'In what you might call a spiritual sense, I mean. A friendship, I mean. Come on, we'll get back to my gaff on the double and soon have you fitted up like the toff you most undoubtedly are!'

Bemused but beginning to feel more hopeful, Jherek Carnelian followed his young friend through a maze of dark and foggy streets until they came at last to a tall, black building which stood by itself at the end of an alley. Several of the windows were lit and from them came sounds of laughter, shouts and, Jherek thought, voices raised in anger.

'Is this your castle, Mr Vine?' he asked.

'Well——' Snoozer Vine grinned at Jherek. 'It is and it isn't, your lordship. I sometimes share it, you might say, with one or two mates. Fellow craftsmen, sir.' He bowed low and gestured elaborately for Jherek to precede him up the broken steps to the main door, a thing of cracked wood and rusted metal, with peeling brown paint and, in its centre, a dirty brass knocker shaped like a lion's head.

They reached the top of the steps.

107

'Is this where we're to stay tonight, Mr Vine?' Jherek looked with interest at the door. It was marvellously ugly.

'No, no. We'll just fit ourselves up here and then go on—in a cab.'

'To Bromley?'

'Bromley later.'

'But I must get to Bromley as soon as possible. You see, I——'

'I know. Love calls. Bromley beckons. Rest assured, you'll be united with your lady tomorrow.'

'You are very certain, Mr Vine.' Jherek was pleased to have found such an omniscient guide in his quest. He was certain that his luck was changing at last.

'I am, indeed. If Snoozer Vine gives a promise, your lordship, it means something.'

'So this place is——?'

'You might call it a sort of extraordinary lodging house—for gentlemen of independent means, sir. For professional ladies. And for children—and others—bent on learning a trade. Welcome, your lordship, to Jones's Kitchen.'

And Snoozer Vine leaned past Jherek and rapped several times with the knocker upon the door.

But the door was already opening. A little boy stood in the shadows of the mephitic hallway. He was dressed entirely in what appeared to be strips of rag. His hair was greasy and long and his face was smeared with grime.

'Otherwise known,' said the boy, sneering up at the pair, 'as the Devil's Arsehole. 'Ello, Snoozer—who's yer mate?'

CHAPTER TWELVE

THE CURIOUS COMINGS AND GOINGS
OF SNOOZER VINE

JONES'S KITCHEN was hot and rich with odours, not all of which Jherek found to his taste. It was packed with people, too. In the long main room on the ground floor and in the gallery above it which ran around the whole place there was crowded a miscellaneous collection of benches, chairs and tables (none in very good condition). Below the gallery and filling the length of one wall was a big bar of stained deal. Opposite this bar, in a huge stone grate, roared a fire over which was being roasted on a spit the carcass of some animal. Dirty straw and offal, rags and papers covered the flagstones of the floor and the floor also swam with liquid of all kinds. Through the permanent drone of voices came, at frequent intervals, great gusts of laughter, bursts of song, whines of accusation and streams of oaths.

Soiled finery was evidently the fashion here tonight.

Powdered, painted ladies in elaborate, tattered hats wore gowns of green, red and blue silk trimmed with lace and embroidery and when they raised their skirts (which was often) they displayed layers of filthy petticoats. Some had the tops of their dresses undone. Men wore whiskers, beards or stubble and had battered top-hats or bowlers on their heads, loud check waistcoats, mufflers, caps, masher overcoats, yellow, blue and brown trousers, and many sported watch-chains or flowers in their button-holes. The girls and boys wore cut down versions of similar clothes and some of the children imitated their elders by painting their faces with rouge and charcoal. Glasses, bottles and mugs were in every hand, even the smallest, and there was a general scattering of plates and knives and forks and scraps of food on the tables and the floor.

Snoozer Vine guided Jherek Carnelian through this press. They all knew Snoozer Vine. 'Wot 'o, Snoozer!' they cried. ' 'Ow yer goin', Snooze,' and 'Give us a kiss, Snoozy!'

And Snoozer grinned and he nodded and he saluted as he steered

Jherek through this Dawn Age crowd, these seeds from which would blossom a profusion of variegated plants which would grow and wilt, grow and wilt through a million or two years of history. These were his ancestors. He loved them all. He, too, smiled and waved and got, he was pleased to note, many a broad smile in return.

The little boy's question was frequently repeated.

''Oo's yer friend, Snoozer?'

'Wot's ther cove inna fancy dress?'

'Wot yer got there, Snooze?'

Once or twice, as he paused to peck a girl on the cheek, Snoozer would look up and answer:

'Foreign gent. Business acquaintance. Easy, easy, yer'll frighten 'im off. 'E's not familiar wiv our customs in this country.' And he would wink at the girl and pass on.

And once someone winked back at Snoozer. 'A new mark, eh? Har, har! You'll be buyin' ther rounds termorrer, eh?'

'Likely,' replied Snoozer, tapping the side of his nose as he had done before.

Jherek reflected that the translation pill was not working at full strength, for he could not understand much of the language, even now. Unfortunately what the pill had probably done was to translate his own vocabulary into 19th century English, rather than supplying him with their vocabulary. Still, he could get by well enough and make himself understood perfectly well.

''Ello, ducks,' said an old lady, patting his bottom as he went by and offering him something in a glass whose smell reminded him of the way the other lady had smelled. 'Want some gin? Want some fun, 'andsome?'

'Clear off, Nellie,' said Snoozer with equanimity. ''E's mine.'

Jherek noticed how Snoozer's voice had changed since he had entered the portals of Jones's Kitchen. He seemed almost to speak two different languages.

Several other women, men and children expressed their willingness to make love to Jherek and he had to admit that on another occasion in different circumstances he would have been pleased to have enjoyed the pleasures offered. But Snoozer dragged him on.

What *was* beginning to puzzle Jherek was that none of these people much resembled in attitude or even appearance Mrs Amelia Underwood. The horrifying possibility came to him that there might be more than one date known as 1896. Or different time-streams

(Brannart Morphail had explained the theory to him once). On the other hand, Bromley was known to Snoozer Vine. There were probably slightly different tribal customs applying in different areas. Mrs Underwood came from a tribe where dullness and misery were in vogue, whereas here the people believed in merrymaking and variety.

Now Snoozer led Jherek up a rickety staircase crowded with people and onto the gallery. A passage ran off the gallery and Snoozer entered it, pushing Jherek ahead of him until they came to one of several doors and Snoozer stopped, taking a key from his waistcoat pocket and opening one of the doors.

Going in, Jherek found himself in pitch darkness.

'Just a minute,' said Snoozer, stumbling around. A scratching sound was followed by a flash of light. Snoozer's face was illuminated by a little fire glowing at the tips of his fingers. He applied this fire to an object of glass and metal which stood on a table. The object began, itself, to glow and gradually brought a rather dim light to the whole small room.

The room contained a bed with rumpled grey sheets, a mahogany wardrobe, a table and two Windsor chairs, a large mirror and about fifty or sixty trunks and suitcases of various sizes. They were stacked everywhere, reaching to the ceiling, poking out from under the bed, teetering on top of the wardrobe, partially obscuring the mirror.

'You collect boxes, Mr Vine?' Jherek admired the trunks. Some were leather, some metal, some wooden. They all looked in excellent condition. Many had inscriptions which Jherek, of course, could not read, but the inscriptions seemed to be of a wide variety.

Snoozer Vine snorted and laughed. 'Yes,' he said. 'That's right, your lordship. My hobby, it is. Now, let's think about your kit.' He began to pace about the room, inspecting the cases, a frown of concentration upon his face. Every so often he would stop, perhaps to wipe some dust off one of his trunks, to peer at the inscription or to test a handle. And then, at last, he pulled two leather travelling bags from under a pile and he stood them beside the lamp on the table, brushing away dust to reveal a couple of hieroglyphics. The bags were matched and the hieroglyphics were also the same.

'Perfect,' said Vine, fingering his sharp chin. 'Excellent, J.C. Your initials, eh?'

'I'm afraid I can't read . . .'

'Don't worry about that. I'll do all the readin' for you. Let's see, we'll need some clothes.'

'Ah!' Jherek was relieved that he could now help his friend. 'Say what you would care to wear, Mr Vine, and I will make it with one of my power rings.'

'Do what?'

'You probably don't have them here,' said Jherek, displaying his rings. 'But with these I can manufacture anything I please—from a —a handkerchief to—um—a house.'

'Come off it!' Snoozer Vine's eyes widened and became wary. 'You a conjurer by trade, then?'

'I can conjure what you want. Tell me.'

Snoozer uttered a peculiar laugh. 'All right. I'll have a pile o' gold —on that table.'

'At once.' With a smile Jherek visualised Snoozer's request and made the appropriate nerve in the appropriate finger operate his ruby power ring. 'There!'

And nothing appeared.

'You're having me on, ain't ya!' Snoozer offered Jherek a sideways look.

Jherek was astonished. 'How odd.'

'Odd's the word,' agreed Snoozer.

Jherek's brow cleared. 'Of course. No energy banks. The banks are a million years in the future.'

'Future?' Snoozer seemed frozen to the spot.

'I am from the future,' said Jherek. 'I was going to tell you later. The ship—well, it's a time machine, naturally. But damaged.'

'Come off it!' Snoozer cleared his throat several times. 'You're a Russian. Or something.'

'I assure you I speak the truth.'

'You mean you could spot the winners of tomorrow's races if I gave you a list tonight?'

'I don't understand.'

'Make predictions—like the fortune-tellers. Is that what you are? A gippo?'

'My predictions wouldn't have much to do with your time. My knowledge of your immediate future is sketchy to say the least.'

'You're a bloody loony,' said Snoozer Vine in some relief, having got over his astonishment. 'An escaped loony. Oh, just my luck!'

'I'm afraid I don't quite . . .'

'Never mind. You still want to get to Bromley?'

'Yes, indeed.'

'And you want to stay at a posh hotel tonight?'

'If that's what you think best.'

'Come on, then,' said Vine. 'We'd better get you the clobber.' He crossed to the wardrobe, shaking his head. 'Cor! You almost had me believing you, then.'

Jherek stood before the mirror and looked at himself with some pleasure. He was dressed in a white shirt with a high, starched collar, a deep purple cravat with a pearl pin, a black waistcoat, black trousers, highly polished black boots, a black frock-coat and on his head a tall, black silk hat.

'The picture of an English aristocrat, though I say it meself,' said Snoozer Vine, who had selected the outfit. 'You'll pass, your lordship.'

'Thank you,' said Jherek, taking his friend's remarks for a compliment. He smiled and fingered the clothes. They reminded him of the clothes Mrs Amelia Underwood had suggested he wear. They cheered him up considerably. They seemed to bring her nearer to him. 'Mr Vine, my dear, they are *charming!*'

'Here, steady on,' said Snoozer, eyeing him with a certain amount of alarm on his thin, quick face. He, himself, was dressed in black, though the costume was not so fine as Jherek's. He picked up the two travelling bags which he had cleaned and filled with several smaller bags. 'Hurry up. The cab'll be here by now. They don't like to hang about long near Jones's.'

They went back through the throng, causing a certain amount of amusement and attracting plenty of cat-calls until they were outside in the cold night. The fog had cleared slightly and Jherek could see a cab waiting in the street. It was of the same type as the one which had knocked him over.

'Victoria Station,' Snoozer told the driver, who sat on a box above and behind the cab.

They got into the hansom and the driver whipped up the horse. They began to rattle through the streets of Whitechapel.

'It's a fair way,' Vine told Jherek, who was fascinated by the cab and what little he could see through the windows. 'We'll change there. Don't want to make the cabby suspicious.'

Jherek wondered why the driver should get suspicious, but he had become used to listening to Snoozer Vine without understanding every word.

Gradually the streets widened out and the gas-lamps became much more frequent. There was a little more traffic, too.

'We're getting near the centre of town,' Snoozer explained when Jherek questioned him. 'Trafalgar Square ahead. This is the Strand. We'll go down Whitehall and then down Victoria Street to the station.'

The names meant nothing to Jherek, but they all had a marvellous, exotic ring to them. He nodded and smiled, repeating the words to himself.

They disembarked outside a fairly large building of concrete and glass which had several tall entrances. Peering through one of the entrances Jherek saw a stretch of asphalt and beyond it a series of iron gates. Beyond the gates stood one or two machines which he recognised immediately as bigger versions of his own locomotive. He cried out in delight. 'A museum!'

'A bleeding railway station,' said Vine. 'This is where the trains go from. Haven't you got trains in your country?'

'Only the one I made myself,' said Jherek.

'Gor blimey!' said Snoozer and raised his eyes towards the glass roof which was supported on metal girders. He hurried Jherek through one of the entrances and across the asphalt so that they passed quite close to a couple of the locomotives.

'What are those other things behind it?' Jherek asked curiously.

'Carriages!' snorted Snoozer.

'Oh, I must make some as soon as I get back to my own time,' Jherek told him.

'Now,' said Snoozer ignoring him, 'you'll have to let me do all the talking. You keep quiet, all right—or you could get us both into trouble.'

'Very well, Snoozer.'

'It's Vine, if you have to address me by name at all. But try not to, see?'

Again, Jherek agreed. They went through an exit where several more cabs were waiting. Snoozer signalled the nearest and they climbed in.

'Imperial Hotel,' said Snoozer. He turned to Jherek who was, again, peering through the window at the romantic night. 'And don't forget what I told you, eh?'

'You are my guide,' Jherek assured him. 'I am in your hands— Vine.'

'Fine.'

And soon the cab had stopped outside a large house whose lower windows blazed with light. There was an imposing entrance, of marble and granite, and a stone awning supported by marble pillars. As the cab drew up a middle-aged man in dark green, wearing a green top-hat taller than Jherek's, rushed from within the building and opened the door. A boy, also in green, but with a pill-box hat on his head, followed the man and took the two bags which the driver handed down.

'Good morning, sir,' said the middle-aged man to Jherek.

'This is Lord Carnell,' said Snoozer Vine. 'I am his man. We telegraphed from Dover to say we'd be arriving about now.'

The middle-aged man frowned. 'I don't recall no wire, sir. But maybe they'll know about it at the reception desk.'

Snoozer paid the driver and they followed the boy with the bags into the warmth of a wide lobby at the far end of which stood a highly polished bar. Behind the bar stood an old man dressed in a black frock-coat with a grey waistcoat. He looked faintly surprised and was leafing through a large book which rested on the bar before him. Jherek glanced about him as Vine approached the bar. There were lots of potted palms in the lobby and these, too, reminded him nostalgically of Mrs Underwood. He hoped he could leave for Bromley early tomorrow.

'Lord Carnell, sir?' the old man in the frock-coat was saying to Vine. 'No telegram, sir, I'm afraid.'

'This is extremely inconvenient,' Vine was saying in still another kind of voice. 'I sent the telegram myself as soon as the boat docked.'

'Not to worry, sir,' the old man soothed, 'we have plenty of unreserved accommodation as it happens. What will you require?'

'A suite,' said Snoozer Vine, 'for his lordship, with a room attached for my use.'

'Of course, sir.' Again the old man consulted the book. 'Number 26, facing the river, sir. A beautiful view.'

'That will do,' Vine said rather haughtily.

'And if you will sign the register, sir.'

Jherek was about to point out that he could not write when Vine picked up the pen, dipped it in the ink and made marks on the paper. Apparently it was not necessary for them both to sign.

They crossed soft, scarlet carpets to a cage of curling brass and iron and the boy pulled back a gate so that they could get in. Another old man stood inside the cage. 'Number 26,' said the boy.

Jherek looked around him. 'A strange sort of room,' he murmured. But Vine didn't reply. He looked steadily away from Jherek.

The old man pulled a rope and suddenly they were rising into the air. Jherek giggled with pleasure and then yelped as he fell against the wall when the cage stopped suddenly. The old man opened the gate.

'Aha,' said Jherek knowingly. This was a crude form of levitation. The gate opened onto a scarlet carpeted hallway. There was an air of great luxury about the whole place. It was more like home.

Jherek and Vine were almost immediately joined by the black-coated man and the boy with their bags. They were ushered a short distance along the hall and into a suite of large rooms. Windows looked out onto a stretch of gleaming water similar to that which Jherek had seen when he first arrived.

'Would you like some supper brought up, sir?' the man in the frock-coat asked Jherek. Jherek realised that he was beginning to feel hungry and he opened his mouth to agree with the suggestion when Snoozer Vine interrupted.

'No, thank you. We have already dined—on the train up from Dover.'

'Then I'll bid you good night, your lordship.' The man in the frock-coat seemed to resent Snoozer Vine's speaking for Jherek. This last remark was directed pointedly at Jherek.

'Good night,' said Jherek. 'And thank you for putting the river there. I——'

'For the view. We've been away for some time. His lordship hasn't seen the good old Thames since last year,' hastily explained Snoozer Vine, herding the old man and the boy before him.

At last the door closed.

Vine gave Jherek a strange look and shook his head. 'Well, I mustn't complain. We're in. And when we go out we'll be a deal better off I shouldn't wonder. You'd better get some kip while you've got the chance. I'll nip into my own room now. Nightie night—your lordship.' Chuckling, Snoozer Vine left the main room and closed a door behind him.

Jherek had understood almost nothing of Vine's final remarks, but he shrugged and went to stare out at the river. He imagined himself in a punt on it with Mrs Amelia Underwood. He imagined Mrs Amelia Underwood here beside him now and he sighed. Even if he had difficulty getting back to his own time he was certain that he could settle here quite easily. Everyone was so kind to him. Perhaps Mrs Underwood would be kinder in her own time. Well, they would soon be reunited. Humming the tune of 'All Things Bright and Beautiful' he padded about the suite, exploring the bedroom, the sitting room, the dressing room and the bathrooms. He already knew about plumbing, but he was fascinated by the taps and the plugs and the chains involved in letting water into and out of various china containers. He played with them all for some time before tiring of it and going back into his gaslit bedroom. Perhaps he had better sleep, he thought. And yet, for all his adventures, his minor injuries, his excitement, he did not feel at all weary.

He wondered if Snoozer were tired. He opened the door to see if his friend had managed to sleep and was surprised to find Vine gone. The bed was empty. The two suitcases were open on the bed but the smaller cases they had contained were also missing.

Jherek could think of no explanation for Snoozer's disappearance and neither could he imagine where Snoozer had taken the bags. He went back into his own room and regarded the Thames again, watching as a black craft chugged by before vanishing under the arch of one of the nearer bridges. The fog was so thin now that Jherek could see to the other side of the river, could see the outlines of the buildings and the glow of the gaslamps. Did Bromley lie in that direction?

He heard a movement from Snoozer's room. He turned. Snoozer had come back, creeping in and closing the outer door quietly behind him. He had two of the smaller bags held in one hand and they were full. They were bulging. He looked a little surprised when he saw Jherek watching him. He gave a weak grin. 'Oh, 'ello, your lordship.'

'Hello, Snoozer.' Jherek did not feel particularly curious about Snoozer's activities. He smiled back.

Snoozer misinterpreted the smile, it seemed. He nodded as he crossed to his bed and put the two small cases into the larger one. 'You guessed, ain't you?'

'About the bags?'

'That's right. Well, there's something in it for you, too.' Snoozer laughed. 'If it's only the fare to Bromley, eh?'

'Ah, yes,' said Jherek.

'Well, o' course, there'll be a cut. A quarter suit you? 'Cause I'm taking all the risks. Mind you, it's the best haul I've ever had. I've dreamed of getting in here for years. Any snoozer would. I needed someone like you who'd pass for a gent, see.'

'Oho,' said Jherek, still unable to get the drift of Snoozer's remarks. He smiled again.

'You're brighter than I thought, you are. I suppose they got hotel snoozers even where you come from, eh? Well, don't worry, as I say. Just keep mum. We'll leave here early in the morning, before anyone else is up—and we'll be a lot richer than they'll be, eh?' Snoozer laughed. He winked. He opened his door and left again, closing the lock carefully.

Jherek went over to the bags. He had some difficulty in working out how they unfastened, but at last he got one open and looked inside. Snoozer seemed to be collecting watches and rings and gold discs. There were various other items in the bags, including some diamond pins very similar to the one in Jherek's cravat (only his was a pearl), some small links for securing the cuffs of shirts, some thin cases which contained white paper tubes which in turn contained some kind of aromatic herb. There were some flasks, in silver and in gold, there were studs and chains and pendants, necklaces and a couple of tiaras and a fan with a frame of gold studded with emeralds. They were all quite pretty but Jherek could not see why Snoozer Vine needed so many things of that kind. He shrugged and closed the bag.

A little while later Snoozer returned with two more bags. He was elated. He was panting. His eyes shone.

'The biggest haul of my life. You wouldn't believe the swag what's here tonight. I couldn't have picked a better night in a hundred years. There's been a big ball in Belgravia somewhere. I saw a programme. And all the nobs from the country have come up—*and* people from abroad—in all their finest. There must be a million quid's worth of stuff lying around in their rooms. And them snoring away and me just taking me pick!' Snoozer removed a large bunch of keys from his pocket and rattled them in Jherek's face. From his other pocket he pulled a small object which reminded Jherek of

118

the club Yusharisp had carried when disguised as a Piltdown Man. Only this one was smaller. 'And look at this! Found it on top of a jewel case. Pearl-handled pistol. I'll keep that for meself,' Snoozer laughed heartily, though very quietly, 'in case o' burglars, eh, Jerry?'

Jherek was glad to see his friend pleased. Other people's enthusiasms were often quite hard to appreciate and this was certainly one he could not share, but he smiled.

'In case o' burglars!' Snoozer repeated in delight. He opened one of the cases and scooped several strands of pearls out, holding them up to the light. 'We'll pack all these away and be out of here while they're still sleeping off the effects of the bubbly. Ha, ha!'

Now Jherek did feel tired. He yawned. He stretched. 'Fine,' he said. 'Have you any objection if I sleep for an hour or two before we leave, Snoozer?'

'Sleep the sleep of the just, my old partner. You brought me luck and that's a fact. I can retire. I can get a stable and stock it with horses and become an Owner. Snoozer Vine, owner of the Derby winner. I can see it there.' He gestured with his hands. 'And I could buy a pub, somewhere out in the country. Hailsham way. Or Epsom, near the track.' He closed his eyes. 'Or go abroad. To Paris! Oo-la-la.' He chuckled to himself as he folded another bag and tucked it under his coat. And then he had left again.

Jherek lay down on his bed, having removed his coat and his silk hat. He was looking forward to dawn when, he hoped, Snoozer would set him on his way to Bromley and Number 23 Collins Avenue.

'Oh, Mrs Underwood,' he breathed. 'Do not fear. Even now your saviour is contemplating your rescue!'

He hoped that Mr Underwood would understand the position.

Jherek was awakened by Snoozer Vine shaking his shoulder. Snoozer had a look of heated rapture upon his face. There was sweat on his brow. His eyes glittered.

'Time to be off, Jerry, me boy. Back to Jones's. We'll have the stuff fenced by tonight and then it's me for the Continent for a bit.'

'Bromley?' said Jherek, sitting stiffly up.

'Bromley as soon as you like. I'll drop you off at the station. I'll get you a ticket. If I had the time I'd have a special bloody train laid on for you after what you've helped me do.'

Snoozer brandished Jherek's top hat and coat. 'Quick, into these. I've already told 'em we're leaving early—for your country estate. They don't suspect a thing. It's funny what a trusting lot o' buggers they are when they think you got a title.'

Jherek Carnelian struggled into the coat. There came a knock at the door. For an instant Snoozer looked wary and agitated and then he relaxed, grinning. 'That'll be the boy for our bags. We'll let him carry the swag out for us, eh?'

Jherek nodded absently. Again he was contemplating his reunion with Mrs Underwood.

The boy came in. He picked up their bags. He frowned as he found he had to struggle with them, as if he was remembering that they had not seemed so heavy the night before.

'Well, sir,' said Snoozer Vine to Jherek Carnelian in a loud voice, 'you'll be pleased to get back to Dorset, I shouldn't wonder.'

'Dorset?' As they followed the boy along the passage Jherek wondered why Vine was looking at him in such a strange way. 'Bromley,' he said.

'That's right, sir.' Anxiously Snoozer put a finger to his lips. They entered the cage and were borne to the ground floor. Vine's expression of elation was still on his face but he was doing his best to hide it, to compose his features into the somewhat sterner lines of the previous night.

It was dawn outside; a grey, rainy dawn. Jherek waited near the door while another boy went to find a cab, for there were none waiting at this time in the morning. The same old man stood behind the reception desk. He was frowning slightly as he accepted the gold discs which Snoozer Vine handed to him.

'His lordship's eager to get back to the country,' Vine was explaining. 'Her ladyship hasn't been well. That is why we returned so suddenly from France.'

'I see.' The old man scribbled on a piece of paper and then handed the paper to Vine.

Jherek thought he detected a somewhat strained atmosphere in the hotel this morning. Everyone seemed to be looking at him with a slightly peculiar expression. He heard the clatter of a cab coming along the street and saw it appear with the green-suited boy clinging to the running board. The middle-aged man in the top hat opened the glass door. The boy picked up the bags as Snoozer crossed the lobby and joined Jherek.

'Good-bye, your lordship,' said the man at the desk.

'Good-bye,' said Jherek cheerfully. 'Thank you.'

'These bags are a weight, sir,' said the boy.

'Don't be cheeky, Herbert,' said the middle-aged man holding the door.

'Yes,' said Jherek conversationally, 'they're full of Snoozer's swag now.'

Snoozer gasped as the mouth of the middle-aged man dropped open.

At that moment a red-faced man in a nightshirt came running down the stairs pulling on a velvet dressing gown that Jherek would have liked to have worn himself.

'I've been robbed!' shouted the red-faced man. 'My wife's jewels. My cigarette case. Everything.'

'Stop!' shouted the old man at the desk.

The middle-aged man let the door go and threw himself at Jherek. The boy dropped the bags. Jherek fell over. He had never been attacked physically before. He laughed.

The middle-aged man turned on Snoozer Vine who was desperately trying to get the bags through the door and out to the cab, a look of profound agony on his thin face. He dropped the bags when the middle-aged man tackled him.

'You can't,' he yelled. 'Not now!' He wriggled free, tugging something from his pocket. 'Stand back!'

'A snoozer!' growled the middle-aged man. 'I should have known. Don't threaten me. I'm an ex-sergeant-major.' And again he dived at Snoozer.

There was a fairly loud bang.

The middle-aged man fell down. Snoozer stared at him in surprise. The surprise was mirrored on the face of the middle-aged man who now had a huge red stain on the front of his green uniform. His top hat fell off. Snoozer waved something at the man in the dressing gown and the old man in the black coat. 'Pick up the bags, Jerry,' he said.

Bemused, Jherek bent and lifted the two heavy bags. The boy was hovering behind one of the potted palms, his cheeks sucked in and his eyes wide. Snoozer Vine's back was to the door but Jherek noticed that the cabby had climbed down from his cab and was running down the street waving to someone whom Jherek couldn't see. He heard a whistle sound.

'Through the door,' said Snoozer in a small, cold voice.

Jherek went through the door and out into the rainy street.

'Into the cab, quick,' said Snoozer. Now he waved the black and silver object at the cabby and another man, dressed in a suit of dark blue and wearing a hat with a rounded crown and no brim, who were running up the street towards them. 'Get back or I'll fire!'

Jherek found the whole thing extremely amusing. He had no idea what was going on but he was enjoying the drama. He looked forward to telling Mrs Amelia Underwood about it in a few hours. He wondered why Snoozer Vine was climbing onto the box of the cab and whipping up the horse. The cab shot off down the street. Jherek heard one more bang and then they had turned a corner and were dashing along another thoroughfare which had a number of people—mainly dressed in grey overcoats and flat hats—in it. All the people turned to stare at the cab as it flew past. Jherek waved gaily to some of them.

Full of elation, for he would soon be in Bromley, he began to sing. 'Jesus bids us shine with a pure, clear light . . .' he sang as he was jolted from side to side in the hurtling cab. 'Like a little candle burning in the night!'

They reached the entrance to Jones's Kitchen some time later, for Snoozer Vine had decided to leave the cab a good mile or so away. Jherek, who was carrying the bags, was quite tired when they got to the house and he wondered why Snoozer's manner had changed so markedly. The man kept snarling at him and saying things like 'You certainly turned good luck into bad in a hurry. I hope to Christ that feller didn't die. If he did it's as much your fault as mine.'

'Die?' Jherek had said innocently. 'But can't he be resurrected? Or is this too early?'

'Shut yer mouth!' Snoozer had told him. 'Well, if I swing so will you. I'd 'ave left yer behind if I 'adn't known you'd blab it all out in two minutes. I ought ter do you in, too.' He laughed bitterly. 'Don't ferget yore an accomplice, that's all.'

'You said you'd get me to Bromley,' Jherek reminded him gently as they went up the steps to Jones's Kitchen.

'Bromley?' Snoozer Vine sneered. 'Ha! You'll be lucky if you don't wind up in Hell now!'

During the next few days Jherek began to understand, even more profoundly than before, what misery was. He found that he was growing a beard quite involuntarily and it itched terribly. He became infested with tiny insects of three or four different varieties and they bit him all over. The clothes which Snoozer Vine had originally given him were taken from him and he was given a few thin rags to wear instead. Snoozer occasionally left the room they both shared and went down to the ground floor, always returning very surly and unsteady and smelling of the stuff which the woman had offered Jherek on his first night in Jones's Kitchen. And it grew very cold. Snoozer would not allow Jherek to go downstairs and warm himself at the fire so Jherek, as he came to understand the nature of cold, came also to understand the nature of hunger and thirst. Initially he made the most of it, savouring every experience, but slowly it began to depress him. And slowly he found himself unable to respond to the novelty of it all. Slowly he was learning to know what fear was. Snoozer was teaching him that. Snoozer would hiss at him sometimes, making incomprehensible threats. Snoozer would growl and snap and strike Jherek who still had no instinct to defend himself. Indeed, the very idea of defence was alien to him. And all the people who had been so friendly when he had first arrived now either ignored him or, like Snoozer, snarled at him if he ventured out of the room. He became thin and mean and dirty. He ceased to despair and began to forget Bromley and even Mrs Amelia Underwood. He began to forget that he had ever known any existence but the squalid, trunk-filled room above Jones's Kitchen.

And then, one morning, there came a great commotion below. Snoozer was still snoring on the bed, having come back in his usual unsteady, argumentative mood, and Jherek was sleeping in his usual place under the table. Jherek woke first but his senses were too dulled by hunger, fatigue and misery for him to make any reaction to the noise. He heard yells, smashing sounds. Snoozer began to stir and open bleary eyes.

'What is it?' Snoozer said thickly. 'If only that bloody fence would turn up. All that stuff and nobody ter touch it 'cause o' that feller dying.' He swung his legs off the bed and swung a kick, automatically, at Jherek. 'Christ, I wish that bloody 'ansom 'ad killed yer that first bloody night.'

This was almost invariably his waking ritual. But this morning he cocked his head as it dawned on him that something was going on downstairs. He reached under his pillow and brought out his pistol. He got off the bed and went to the door. Cautiously, he opened the door, the pistol in his hand. Again he paused to listen. Loud voices. Oaths. Screams. Women's voices shouting in offended tones. A boy wailing. The deep, aggressive voices of men.

Snoozer Vine, looking little healthier than Jherek, began to pad along the passage. Jherek got up and watched from the doorway. He saw Snoozer reach the gallery just as two men, in the blue clothes he had seen on the other man as they left the hotel, rushed at him from both sides, as if they had been waiting for him. There was another shot. One of the men in blue staggered back. Snoozer broke free of the other's grasp, reached the rail of the gallery, hesitated and then leapt over it to vanish from Jherek's sight.

Jherek began to shuffle along the passage to where one of the men in blue was helping the other get to his feet.

'Stand back!' shouted the one who was not wounded. But Jherek hardly heard him. He shuffled to the rail of the gallery and looked down. He saw Snoozer on the dirty flagstones of the ground floor. His head was bleeding. His whole face seemed covered in blood. He was spreadeagled at an awkward angle and he kept trying to raise himself on his hands and knees and failing. Slowly he was being surrounded by many other men, all dressed in the same blue suits with the same blue hats on their heads. They stood and looked at him, not trying to help him as he made effort after effort to raise himself up. And then he was still.

A fat man—one of the men who served behind the bar in Jones's Kitchen—appeared at the edge of the circle of men in blue. He looked down at Snoozer. He looked up at the gallery and saw Jherek. He pointed. 'That's 'im,' he said. 'That's the other one.'

Jherek felt a strong hand grip his thin shoulder. He was sensitive to pain, for Snoozer had raised a bruise on the same shoulder the night before. But the pain seemed to stimulate his memory. He turned to look up at the grim-faced man who held him.

'Mrs Amelia Underwood,' said Jherek in a small, pleading voice, '23 Collins Avenue, Bromley, Kent, England.'

He repeated the phrase over and over again as he was led down the steps of the gallery, through the deserted main room, out of the door into the morning light where a black waggon drawn by four black horses awaited him. Free from Snoozer, free from Jones's Kitchen, Jherek felt a mindless surge of relief.

'Thank you,' he told one of the men who had climbed into the waggon with him. 'Thank you.'

The man gave a thin smile. 'Don't thank me, lad. They'll 'ang you fer this one, certain.'

CHAPTER THIRTEEN

THE ROAD TO THE GALLOWS: OLD FRIENDS
IN NEW GUISES

BETTER fed, better clothed, and better treated in prison than in Jones's Kitchen, Jherek Carnelian began to recover something of his previous state of mind. He particularly liked the grey baggy suit with the broad arrows stitched all over it and he determined, if he ever got back to his own age, to make himself one rather in the same fashion (though probably with orange arrows). The world of the prison did not have very much colour in it. It was mainly bleak greens and greys and blacks. Even the flesh of the other inmates was somewhat grey. And the sounds, too, had a certain monotony— clangs, cries and curses, for the most part. But the daily ritual of rising, eating, exercising, retiring had a healing effect on Jherek's mind. He had been accused of various crimes in the opening ritual and, save for an occasional visitor who seemed sympathetic, had been left pretty much to himself. He began to think clearly of Bromley again and Mrs Amelia Underwood. He hoped that they would let him out soon, or complete the ritual in whatever way they saw fit. Then he could continue his quest.

Every few days a man in a black suit with a white collar at his throat, carrying a black book, would visit Jherek's white-tiled cell and talk to Jherek about a friend of his who died and another friend of his who was invisible. Jherek found that listening to the man, whose name was Reverend Lowndes, had a pleasant soporific effect and he would smile and nod and agree whenever it seemed tactful to agree or shake his head whenever it seemed that Reverend Lowndes wanted him to disagree. This caused Reverend Lowndes to express great pleasure and smile a great deal and talk in his rather high-pitched and monotonous voice even more about his dead friend and the invisible friend whom, it emerged, was the dead friend's father.

And once, upon leaving, Reverend Lowndes patted Jherek's shoulder and said to him:

'There is no question in my mind that your salvation is at hand.'

This cheered Jherek up and he looked forward to his release. The air outside the prison grew warmer, too, which was pleasant.

Jherek's other visitor was dressed in a black coat and had a silk hat, wing collar and black cravat. His waistcoat was also black, but his trousers were made up of thin grey stripes. He had introduced himself as Mr Griffiths, Defence Counsel. He had a large, dark head and huge, bushy black eyebrows which met near the bridge of his nose. His hands, too, were large and they were clumsy as they handled the documents which he removed from his small leather case. He sat on the edge of Jherek's hard bunk and leafed through the papers, puffing out his cheeks every so often and letting a loud sigh escape his lips from time to time. Then, at last, he turned to Jherek and pursed his lips again before speaking.

"We are going to have to plead insanity, my friend,' he said.

'Ah,' said Jherek uncomprehendingly.

'Yes, indeed. It appears you have admitted everything to the police. Several witnesses have positively identified you. You, indeed, recognised the witnesses before *other* witnesses. You have claimed no mitigating circumstances save that "you were not sure what was going on". That, in itself, is scarcely credible, from the rest of your statement. You saw the dead man, Vine, bringing in his "swag". You helped him carry it about. You escaped with him after he had shot the porter. When questioned as to your name and origins you concocted some wild story about coming from the future in some sort of machine and you gave a name that was evidently invented but which you have insisted upon retaining. That is where I intend to begin *my* case—and that is what might well save your life. Now, you had best tell me, in your own opinion, what happened from the night that you met Alfred Vine until the morning when the police traced you both to Jones's Kitchen and Vine was killed while trying to escape . . .'

Jherek happily told his story to Mr Griffiths, since it passed the time. But Mr Griffiths blew out his cheeks a lot and rolled his eyes once or twice beneath his black eyebrows and once he clapped his hand to his forehead and let forth an oath.

'The only problem I have,' Mr Griffiths said, when he left the first time, 'is in convincing the Jury that a man as apparently sane as yourself in one way is without question a raving lunatic in another. Well, at least I am convinced of the truth of my case. Good-bye, Mr—um . . . good-bye.'

'I hope to see you again soon,' said Jherek politely as the guard let Mr Griffiths out of the cell.

'Yes, yes,' said Mr Griffiths hastily. 'Yes, yes.'

Mr Griffiths made a number of other visits, as did Reverend Lowndes. But whereas Reverend Lowndes always seemed to depart in an even happier mood than formerly, Mr Griffiths usually left with a wild, unhappy look upon his dark face and his manner was always flustered.

The Trial of Jherek Carnelian for his part in the murder of Edward Frank Morris, porter employed by the Imperial Hotel, Piccadilly, in the Borough of Westminster, London, on the morning of April 5th Eighteen Hundred and Ninety Six at approximately Six o'Clock, took place at the Old Bailey Number One Court at 10 a.m. on the 30th May. Nobody, including the Defendant, expected the trial to be a long one. The only speculation concerned the sentence and the sentence, even, did not seem to concern Jherek Carnelian, who had insisted on retaining the made up name in spite of all warnings that refusal to give his own name would go against him. Before the trial began Jherek was escorted to a wooden box in which he had to stand for the duration of the proceedings. He was rather amused by the box, which commanded a view of the rest of a comparatively large room. Mr Griffiths approached the box and spoke to Jherek urgently for a moment.

'This Mrs Underwood. Have you known her for long?'

'A fairly long time,' said Jherek. 'Strictly speaking of course—I *will* know her for a long time.' He laughed. 'I love these paradoxes, don't you.'

'I do not,' said Mr Griffiths feelingly. 'Would she be a respectable woman? I mean, would you say that she was—well—sane, for instance?'

'Eminently.'

'Hmph. Well, I intend to call her, if possible. Have her vouch for your peculiarities—your delusions and so on.'

'Call her? Bring her here, you mean?'

'Exactly.'

'That would be splendid, Mr Griffiths!' Jherek clapped his hands with pleasure. 'You are very kind, sir.'

'Hmph,' said Griffiths, turning away and going back to the table at which he sat with a number of other men all dressed like himself in black gowns and odd-looking false hair which was white and tightly curled with a little tuft hanging down behind. Further back were rows of seats in which sat a number of men in a variety of clothes, with no false hair on their heads. And above and behind Jherek was a gallery containing more people in their ordinary clothes. To his left was another series of tiered benches on which, as he watched, twelve people arranged themselves. All showed a marked interest in him. He was flattered to be the centre of attention. He waved and smiled but, oddly enough, nobody smiled back at him.

And then someone shouted something Jherek didn't catch and everyone suddenly began getting to their feet as another group of men in long robes and false hair filed into the room and sat down behind a series of desks immediately opposite Jherek on the far side of the chamber. It was then that Jherek gasped in astonishment as he recognised the man who seemed to take pride of place, after himself, in the court.

'Lord Jagged of Canaria!' he cried. 'Have you followed me through time? What a friend you are, indeed!'

One of the men in blue who stood behind Jherek leaned forward and tapped him on the shoulder. 'Be quiet, lad. You speak when you're spoken to.'

But Jherek was too delighted to listen to him.

'Lord Jagged! Don't you recognise me?'

Everyone had begun to sit down again and Lord Jagged did not seem to have heard Jherek. He was leafing through some papers which someone had placed before him.

'Quiet!' said the man behind Jherek again.

Jherek turned with a smile. 'It's my friend,' he explained, pointing.

'You'd better hope so,' said the man grimly. 'That's the Lord Chief Justice, that is. He's your Judge, lad—Lord Jagger. Don't get on the wrong side of him or you haven't a chance.'

'Lord *Jagged*,' said Jherek.

'Silence!' someone cried. 'Silence in court!'

Lord Jagged of Canaria looked up then. He had a peculiar, stern expression on his face and, as he looked at Jherek, he gave no sign that he recognised him.

Jherek was puzzled but guessed that this was some new game of Lord Jagged's. He decided to play it in the same way, so he made no further reference to the indisputable fact that the man opposite him, who seemed to command the respect of all, was his old friend.

The trial began and Jherek's interest remained lively throughout as a succession of people, most of whom he had seen at the hotel, came to tell what had happened on the night when Jherek and Snoozer Vine had arrived at the Imperial and what subsequently took place on the following morning. These people were questioned by a man called Sir George Freeman and then Mr Griffiths would question them again. By and large the people recounted the events pretty much as Jherek remembered them, but Mr Griffiths did not seem to believe them much of the time. Mr Griffiths was also interested in their view of Jherek. Had he behaved oddly? Did they notice anything strange about his face? What had he said? Some of the people remembered that Jherek had said some strange things—or at least things which they had not understood. They believed now that this was a thieves' code arranged between Jherek and Snoozer Vine. Men in blue uniforms were questioned, including the one whom Jherek had seen in the street when he left the hotel and several of the ones who had come to Jones's Kitchen later. Again these were closely questioned by Mr Griffiths. The Reverend Lowndes appeared to talk about Jherek and told everybody that he thought Jherek had 'repented'.

Then there was a break for lunch and Jherek was escorted back to a small, clean cell and given some unappetising food to eat. As he ate, Mr Griffiths came to see him again.

'There's every chance, I think, that the Jury will find you guilty but insane,' Mr Griffiths told him.

Jherek nodded absently. He was still thinking of the surprise at seeing Lord Jagged in the court. How had his friend managed to find him? How, for that matter, had he been able to get back through time? In another time machine? Jherek hoped so, for it would make everything much easier. As soon as all this was over he would take Mrs Amelia Underwood back with Lord Jagged in the new time machine. He would be quite glad to get back to his own age, for this one was, after a while, a bit tedious.

'Particularly,' Mr Griffiths went on, 'since you did not actually shoot the man. On the other hand, the prosecution seems out for blood and the Jury doesn't look too sympathetic. It'll probably be up to the Judge. Lord Jagger's got a reputation for leniency, I hear . . .'

'Lord *Jagged*,' Jherek told Mr Griffiths. 'That's his real name, at any rate. He's a friend of mine.'

'So that's what that was all about.' Mr Griffiths shook his head. 'Well, anyway, you're helping prove my case.'

'He's from my own period,' Jherek said. 'My closest friend in my own age.'

'He's rather well-known in *our* age,' said Mr Griffiths with a crooked smile. 'The most brilliant Q.C. in the Empire, the youngest Lord Chief Justice ever to sit on the bench.'

'So this is where he used to go on those long trips!' Jherek laughed. 'I wonder why he never mentioned it to me?'

'I wonder!' Mr Griffiths snorted and got up. 'Your lady friend is here, by the way. She had read about the case in the papers this morning and contacted me herself.'

'Mrs Underwood! This is wonderful. *Two* old friends. Oh, thank you, Mr Griffiths!' Jherek sprang to his feet as the door opened and revealed the woman he loved.

She was so beautiful in her dark velvet clothes. Her hat was quite plain with a little veil coming down in front of it through which he could see her lovely, heart-shaped face.

'Mrs Amelia Underwood!' Jherek moved forward to embrace her, but she withdrew.

'Sir!'

A warder made a gesture, as if to assist her.

'It's all right now,' said Mrs Underwood to the warder. 'Yes, it is he, Mr Griffiths.' She spoke very distantly and sadly as if she remembered a dream of which Jherek had been part.

'We can leave here and return very soon!' Jherek assured her. 'Lord Jagged is here. He must have a time machine. We can all go back in it.'

'I cannot go back, Mr Carnelian.' She spoke in a low voice, in the same remote tone. 'And until I saw you a moment ago I did not quite believe I had ever been there. How did you get here?'

'I followed you. In a time-machine supplied by Brannart Morphail. I knew that you loved me.'

'Love? Ah . . .' She sighed.

'And you still love me, I can tell.'

'No!' She was shocked. 'I am married. I am . . .' She recovered herself. 'I did not come for this, Mr Carnelian. I came to see if it really were you and, if so, to plead for your life. I know that you would do nothing as wicked as take part in a murder—or even a robbery. I am sure you were duped. You were ever naïve in some ways. Mr Griffiths wants me to tell a lie to the court which, he thinks, might save your life.'

'A lie?'

'He wants me to say that I have known you for some time and that you always displayed idiotic tendencies.'

'Must you say that? Why not tell them the truth?'

'They will not believe the truth. No one would!'

'I have noticed that they tend to ignore me when I tell them the truth and listen only when I repeat back to them what they have *told* me is the truth.'

Now Mr Griffiths was looking from Jherek to Mrs Amelia Underwood and back again and there was a miserable, haunted look on his face. 'You mean you both believe this wild nonsense about the future?'

'It is not nonsense, Mr Griffiths,' said Mrs Amelia Underwood firmly. 'But, on the other hand, I do not ask *you* to believe it. The important thing is to save Mr Carnelian's life—even if it means going against all my principles and uttering a perjury to the Court. It seems the only way, in this instance, to stop an injustice taking place!'

'Yes, yes,' said Mr Griffiths desperately. 'So you will go into the witness box and tell the jury that Mr—Carnelian—is mad. That is all I shall require.'

'Yes,' she whispered.

'You do love me,' said Jherek, also speaking softly. 'I can see it in your eyes, Mrs Underwood.'

She looked at him once, a look of longing, of agony. An imploring look. And then she turned and had left the cell.

'She does love me!' Jherek skipped around the cell. Mr Griffiths watched him skip. Mr Griffiths seemed tired. He had an air of fatalism about him as he, too, left the cell and Jherek began to sing at the top of his voice. 'All things bright and beautiful, all creatures great and small. All things wise and wonderful . . .'

After lunch everyone assumed their places again and the first person to appear was Mrs Amelia Underwood, looking even more strained than ever, in the role of Witness for the Defence.

Mr Griffiths asked her if she had known Jherek before. She said she had met him when travelling with her missionary father in South

America, that he had caused her some embarrassment but that he was 'harmless'.

'An idiot, would you say, Mrs Underwood?'

'Yes,' murmured Mrs Underwood, 'an idiot.'

'Something of—um—an innocent, eh?'

'An innocent,' she agreed in the same voice. 'Yes.'

'Did he show any violent tendencies?'

'None. I do not believe he knows what violence is.'

'Very good. And crime? Would you say he had any notion of crime?'

'None.'

'Excellent.' Mr Griffiths turned towards the twelve men who were all leaning forward, concentrating on the exchange. 'I think, members of the jury that this lady—the daughter of a missionary—has successfully proved to you that not only did the defendant not *know* he was being involved in a crime by the deceased Alfred Vine but that he was incapable knowingly of committing any crime. He came to England to seek out the woman who had been kind to him in his own country—in the Argentine, as Mrs Underwood has told you. He was duped by unscrupulous rogues into aiding them in a theft. Knowing nothing of our customs . . .'

Lord Jagger leaned forward. 'I think we can save all this for the summing up, Mr Griffiths.'

Mr Griffiths bowed his head. 'Very well, m'lud. I apologise.'

And now it was Sir George Freeman's turn to question Mrs Underwood. He had small beady eyes, a red nose and an aggressive manner. He asked Mrs Underwood for particulars of where and when she had met Mr Carnelian. He produced arguments and evidence to show that no ship had docked in London from the Argentine on the date mentioned. He suggested that Mrs Underwood had misguidedly felt sorry for Mr Carnelian and had come forward to give evidence which was untrue in order to save him. Was she one of those who objected to capital punishment? He could understand that many good Christians were. He did not suggest that she was appearing in the witness box from anything but the best—if most misguided —of motives. And so on and so on until Mrs Underwood burst into tears and Jherek tried to climb out of his own box and go to her.

'Mrs Underwood!' he cried. 'Just tell them what really happened. Lord Jagged will understand! He will tell them that you are speaking the truth!'

And then everyone seemed to be springing up at once and there was a loud babble of voices and the rapping of a hammer against wood and a man crying loudly:

'Silence in court! Silence in court!'

'I shall have to have the court cleared in the event of a further demonstration of this kind,' said Lord Jagger drily.

'But she is only lying because these people will not believe the truth!' cried Jherek.

'Silence!'

Jherek looked wildly around him. 'They said that you would not believe the truth—that we met a million years in the future, that I followed her back here because I loved her—still do love her . . .'

Lord Jagger ignored Jherek and instead leaned towards the men in the false hair below him. 'The witness may leave the box,' he said. 'She seems to be in distress. Do you have any further questions, gentlemen?'

Mr Griffiths shook his head in silent despair. Sir George Freeman seemed quietly pleased and also shook his head.

Jherek watched Mrs Underwood being led from the box. He saw her disappear and he had a terrible feeling that he would never see her again. He looked appealingly at Lord Jagger.

'Why did you let them make her cry, Jagged?'

'Silence!'

'I think I have successfully proven, m'lud, that the only witness for the defence was lying,' said Sir George Freeman.

'Have you anything to say to that, Mr Griffiths?' Lord Jagger asked.

Mr Griffiths had lowered his head. 'No, m'lud.' He turned and looked at Jherek, who was still agitated. 'Though I believe we have had ample proof of the defendant's unbalanced mental state today.'

'We shall decide on that later,' said Lord Jagger. 'And it is not, I should like to remind the jury, the defendant's mental condition *today* which is being examined. We are trying to discover whether he was mad on the morning of the murder.'

'Lord Jagged!' cried Jherek. 'I beg you. Finish this thing now. The charade might have been amusing to begin with, but it has caused Mrs Underwood genuine grief. Perhaps you do not understand how these people feel—but I do—I have experienced quite awful emotions and states of mind myself since I have been here.'

'Silence!'

'Lord Jagged!'

'Silence!'

'You will be able to speak in your own defence later, if you wish,' said Lord Jagger, without a flicker of humour, without a single sign of recognition. And Jherek at last began to doubt that this was his friend on the bench. Yet the face, the mannerisms, the voice were all the same—and the name was almost the same. It could not be a coincidence.

And then the thought occurred to him that Lord Jagged was taking some malicious pleasure in the proceedings—that he was not Jherek's friend at all. That he had engineered this entire fiasco from start to finish.

The rest of the trial seemed to take place in a flash. And when Lord Jagger asked Jherek if he wished to speak, he merely shook his head. He was too depressed to make any reaction, to try to convince them of the truth. He began to believe that, possibly, he was, indeed, quite mad.

But the thought almost made Jherek dizzy. It could not be! It could not be!

And then Lord Jagger made a short speech to the jury and they all left the court again. Jherek was taken back to his cell and was joined by Mr Griffiths.

'It looks grim,' said Mr Griffiths. 'You should have kept quiet, you know. Now they all think it was an elaborate trick to get you off. This could ruin me.'

He took something from his case and handed it to Jherek. 'Your friend, Mrs Underwood, asked me to give you this.'

Jherek took the paper. He looked at the marks on it and then handed it back to Mr Griffiths. 'You had better read it.'

Mr Griffiths squinted at the paper. He blushed. He coughed. 'It's rather personal.'

'Please read it,' said Jherek.

'Well, here goes—ahem—"I blame myself for what has happened. I know they will put you in prison for a long time, if they do not hang you. I fear that you have little hope now of acquittal and so I must tell you, Jherek, that I do love you, that I miss you, that I shall always remember you." Hmph. It's unsigned. Very wise. Most indiscreet to write it at all.'

Jherek was smiling again. 'I knew she loved me. I'll think of a way to rescue her, even if Lord Jagged will not help me.'

'My dear boy,' said Mr Griffiths solemnly, 'you must try to remem-

ber the seriousness of your position. It is very much on the cards
that they will sentence you to be hanged.'

'Yes?' said Jherek. 'By the way, Mr Griffiths, what's involved in
this "hanging", can you tell me?'

And Mr Griffiths sighed, got up and left the cell without a further word.

Jherek was escorted back to his box for the third time. As he
mounted the steps he saw Lord Jagger and the others taking their
places.

The twelve men came in and resumed their seats.

An oppressive silence now hung over the room.

One of the men in false hair began to read from a list of names
and every time he read a name one of the twelve would answer
'Aye', until all twelve names had been read.

Then the man next to him got up and addressed the twelve. 'Gentlemen of the Jury, have you agreed upon your verdict?'

One of the twelve answered, 'Yes.'

'Do you find the prisoner at the bar guilty or not guilty?'

For a moment all twelve turned their eyes on Jherek whose attention was scarcely on the ritual at all.

'Guilty.'

Jherek was startled as the hands of the two warders fell simultaneously upon his shoulders. He looked at each of their faces
curiously.

Lord Jagger looked steadily into Jherek's eyes.

'Have you anything to say why sentence should not be passed
upon you?'

Jherek said wearily: 'Jagged, I am tired of this farce. Let us take
Mrs Amelia Underwood and go home.'

'I gather you have nothing to say,' said Lord Jagger, ignoring
Jherek's suggestion.

One of the men near Lord Jagger handed Lord Jagger a square
of black cloth which he placed carefully on top of his white false
hair. Reverend Lowndes appeared beside Lord Jagger. He was wearing a long black gown. He looked much sadder than usual.

'You have been found guilty of causing the cruel murder of an
innocent employee of the hotel you sought to rob,' droned Lord
Jagger, and for the first time Jherek thought he saw the light of

humour in his friend's eyes. It was a joke after all. He smiled back.
'And therefore I must sentence you——'

'Ha! Ha!' shouted Jherek. 'It *is* you, Jagged!'

'Silence!' cried someone.

Lord Jagger's voice continued through the confusion, the faint
murmur of voices in the court, until it concluded 'And may the Lord
have mercy on your soul.'

And Reverend Lowndes said:

'Amen!'

And the warders tugged at Jherek to make him leave.

'I will see you later, Jagged!' he called.

But again Jagger ignored him, turning his back as he rose from
his seat and muttering something to the Reverend Lowndes who
nodded mournfully.

'No threats. They won't do you any good,' said one of the warders.
'Come on, son.'

Jherek laughed as he let them lead him back to his cell. 'Really,
I'm losing my sense of humour—my sense of drama. It must have
been that terrible time in Jones's Kitchen. I will apologise to Jagged
as soon as I meet him again!'

'You won't be meeting *him*,' said the warder with a jerk of his
thumb backward, 'until he joins you down there!' And he pointed
at the ground.

'Is that where you think the future lies?' asked Jherek with genuine curiosity.

But they said nothing more to him and in a moment he was alone
in his cell fingering the note which Mrs Amelia Underwood had
sent him, wishing he could read it, but remembering every word.
She loved him. She had said so! He had never experienced such happiness before.

After he had been taken to yet another prison in another black
carriage, Jherek found that he was being treated with even more
kindness than before. The warders who had spoken to him previ-
ously with a sort of surly good humour now spoke with sympathy
and often patted him on the shoulder. Only on the matter of his release did they preserve a silence. One or two would tell him that they
thought 'he ought to have got off' and that 'it wasn't fair', but he
was never able to interpret the significance of their remarks. He

saw Reverend Lowndes quite frequently and was able to make him happy enough. Sometimes they sang one or two hymns together and Jherek was reminded with greater clarity that he would soon be seeing Mrs Amelia Underwood again and singing those same hymns with her. He asked Reverend Lowndes if he had heard anything of Mrs Underwood, but Reverend Lowndes had not.

'She risked much to speak in your defence,' said Reverend Lowndes one day. 'It was in all the newspapers. It is possible that she has compromised herself. I understand that she is a married woman.'

'I understand that,' agreed Jherek. 'But I suppose she is waiting for me to arrange our transport back to my own time.'

'Yes, yes,' said Reverend Lowndes sadly.

'I would have thought that Lord Jagged would have contacted me by now, but perhaps his own time machine is in need of repair,' Jherek mused.

'Yes, yes, yes.' Reverend Lowndes opened his black book and began to read, his lips moving. Then he closed the book and looked up. 'It is tomorrow morning, you know.'

'Oh? You have heard from Lord Jagged?'

'Lord Jagger passed the sentence, if that is what you mean. He named the day as tomorrow. I am glad you are so composed.'

'Why should I not be? That is splendid news.'

'I am sure that the Lord knows how best to judge you.' Reverend Lowndes raised his grey eyes towards the roof. 'You have no need to fear.'

'None at all. Although the ride might be a rough one.'

'Yes, indeed. I understand your meaning.'

'Ah!' Jherek leaned back on his bunk. 'I am looking forward to seeing all my friends again.'

'I am sure they will all be there.' Reverend Lowndes got up. 'I will come early tomorrow morning. If you find it hard to sleep, the warders will join you in your cell.'

'I shall sleep very well, I'm sure. So my release is due around dawn?'

'At eight o'clock.'

'Thank you for the news, Reverend Lowndes.'

Reverend Lowndes's eyes seemed to be watering, but he could not be crying, for there was a smile on his face. 'You do not know what this means to me, Mr Carnelian.'

'I am only too pleased to be able to cheer you up, Reverend Lowndes.'

'Thank you. Thank you.' The Reverend left the cell.

Next morning Jherek was given a rather heavy breakfast, which he ate with some difficulty so as not to offend the warders, who plainly thought they had brought him a special treat. All of them looked sad, however, and kept shaking their heads.

The Reverend Lowndes turned up early, as he had said he would.

'Are you ready?' he asked Jherek.

'More than ready,' Jherek replied cheerfully.

'Would you like to join me in a prayer?'

'If that is what you want, of course.' Jherek knelt down with Reverend Lowndes as he had often knelt before and repeated the words which Reverend Lowndes spoke. This time the prayer seemed to go on for longer than usual and Reverend Lowndes's voice kept breaking. Jherek waited patiently every time this happened. After all what did a few minutes mean when he would soon be reunited with the woman he loved (not to mention his dearest friend)?

And then they left the cell, with a warder on either side, and walked out into an unfamiliar forecourt which was surrounded on all sides by high blank walls. There was a sort of wooden dais erected in the forecourt and above this a tall beam supporting another horizontal beam. From the horizontal beam depended a thick rope with a loop at the bottom end. Another man, in stout black clothes, stood on the dais. Steps led up to it on one side. There was also a lever, near the man in black. Several other people were already in the forecourt. They, too, looked sad. Doubtless they had grown to like Jherek (even though he could not remember having seen several of them before) and did not want him to leave their time.

'Is that the machine?' Jherek asked Reverend Lowndes. He had never expected to see a *wooden* time machine, but he supposed that they used wood for a lot of things in the Dawn Age cultures.

Silently, Reverend Lowndes nodded.

'I go up these steps, do I?'

'You do.'

Reverend Lowndes accompanied Jherek as he climbed the steps. The man in black drew Jherek's hands behind him and tied them securely.

'I suppose this is necessary?' Jherek remarked to the man in black, who had said nothing up to now. 'I had a rubber suit last time.'

The man in black did not reply but turned to Reverend Lowndes instead. 'He's a cool one. It's usually the foreigners scream and kick.'

Reverend Lowndes did not reply. He watched the man in black tie Jherek's feet.

Jherek laughed as the man in black put the rough rope loop over his head and tightened it around his neck. The strands of the loop tickled.

'Well,' he said. 'I'm ready. When are Lord Jagged and Mrs Underwood arriving?'

Nobody replied. Reverend Lowndes murmured something. One of the people in the small crowd below droned a few words.

Jherek yawned and looked up at the blue sky and the rising sun. It was a beautiful morning. He had rather missed the open air of late.

Reverend Lowndes took out his black book and began to read. Jherek turned to ask if Lord Jagged and Mrs Underwood would be long, but then the man in black placed a bag over his head and his voice was muffled and he could no longer see anyone. He shrugged. They would be along soon, he was sure.

He heard the Reverend Lowndes finish speaking. He heard a click and then the floor gave way beneath his feet. The sensation was not very different from that which he had had when travelling here in the time sphere. And then it seemed he was falling, falling, falling, and he ceased to think at all.

CHAPTER FOURTEEN

A FURTHER CONVERSATION WITH THE
IRON ORCHID

THE first thing Jherek considered as he came back to consciousness was that he had a very sore throat. He reached up to touch it, but his hands were still tied behind him. He disseminated the ropes and freed his hands and feet. His neck was chafed and raw. He opened his eyes and looked directly into the tattered, multi-hued face of old Brannart Morphail.

Brannart was grinning. 'I told you so, Jherek. I told you so! And the time machine didn't come back with you. Which means you've lost me an important piece of equipment!' His glee denied his accusations.

Jherek glanced about the laboratory. It was exactly the same as when he had left. 'Perhaps it broke up?' he suggested. 'It *was* made of wood, you know.'

'Wood? Wood? Nonsense. Why are you so hoarse?'

'There was a rope involved. A very primitive machine, all in all. Still, I'm back. Did Lord Jagged come to see you after I'd set off. Did he borrow another time machine?'

'Lord Jagged?'

My Lady Charlotina drifted over. She was wearing the same lily-coloured gown she had worn when he had left. 'Lord Jagged hasn't been here, Jherek, my juice. After all, you'd barely gone before you returned again.'

'It proves the Morphail Effect conclusively,' said Brannart in some satisfaction. 'If one goes back to an age where one does not belong, then so many paradoxes are created that the age merely spits out the intruder as a man might spit out a pomegranate pit which has lodged in his throat.'

Again, Jherek fingered his own throat. 'It took some time to spit me out, however,' he said feelingly. 'I was there for some sixty days.'

'Oh, come now!' Brannart glared at him.

'And Lord Jagged of Canaria was there, too. And Mrs Amelia

Underwood. They seemed to have no difficulty in, as it were, sticking.' Jherek stood up. He was wearing the same grey suit with the broad black arrows on it. 'And look at this. They gave me this suit.'

'It's a beautiful suit, Jherek,' said My Lady Charlotina. 'But you *could* have made it yourself, you know.'

'Power rings don't work in the past. The energy won't transmit,' Jherek told her.

Brannart frowned. 'What was Jagged doing in the past?'

'Some scheme of his own, I take it, which hardly involved me. I understood that he would be returning with me.' Jherek inspected the laboratory, looking in every corner. 'They said Mrs Underwood would join me.'

'Well, she isn't here, yet.' My Lady Charlotina's couch drifted closer. 'Did you enjoy yourself in the Dawn Age?'

'It was often amusing,' Jherek admitted, 'though there were moments when it was quite dull. And other moments when . . .' And for the third time he fingered the marks on his throat. 'Do you know, Lady Charlotina, that many of their pastimes are not pursued from *choice* at all!'

'How do you mean?' She leaned forward to peer at his neck. She reached out to touch the marks.

'Well, it is difficult to explain. Difficult enough to grasp. I didn't understand at first. They grow old—they decay, of course. They have no control over their bodies and barely any over their minds. It is as if—as if they dream perpetually, moved by impulses of which they have no objective understanding. Or, of course, that could be my subjective analysis of their culture, but I don't think so.'

My Lady Charlotina laughed. 'You'll never succeed in explaining it to me, Jherek. I have no brains, merely imagination. A good sense of drama, too.'

'Yes . . .' Jherek had forgotten the part she had played in bringing about the most recent events in his life. But so much time had passed for him that he could not feel any great bitterness towards her any more. 'I wonder when Mrs Amelia Underwood will come.'

'She said she would return?'

'I gathered that Lord Jagged was bringing her back.'

'Are you sure you saw Jagged there?' Brannart asked insistently. 'There has been no record of a time machine either coming or going.'

'There must be a record of one coming,' Jherek said reasonably. 'For *I* returned, did I not?'

'It wasn't really necessary for you to use a machine—the Morphail Effect dealt with you.'

'Well, I was sent in a machine.' Jherek frowned. He was beginning to review the most recent events of his own past. 'At least I *think* it was a time machine. I wonder if I misinterpreted what they were trying to tell me?'

'It is quite possible, I should think,' put in My Lady Charlotina, 'after all, you said yourself how difficult it was to grasp their conception of quite simple matters.'

A musing look crossed Jherek's face. 'But one thing is certain . . .' He took Mrs Amelia Underwood's letter from his pocket, remembering the words which Mr Griffiths had read out to him, 'I love you, I miss you, I shall always remember you.' He touched the crumpled paper to his lips. 'She wants to come back to me.'

'There is every chance that she *will*,' said Brannart Morphail, 'whether she desires it or not. The Morphail Effect. It never fails.' He laughed. 'Not that she will necessarily come to this time again. You might have to search through the whole of the past million years for her. I don't advise that, of course. It could mean disaster for you. You've been very lucky to escape this time.'

'She will find me,' said Jherek happily. 'I know she will. And when she comes I will have built her a beautiful replica of her own age so that she need never pine for home.' He continued, confidentially, to tell Brannart Morphail of his plans. 'You see, I've spent a considerable amount of time in the Dawn Age. I'm intimately acquainted with their architecture and many of their customs. Our world will never have seen anything like the creations I shall make. It will amaze you all!'

'Ah, Jherek!' cried My Lady Charlotina in delight. 'You are beginning to sound like your old self again. Hurrah!'

Some days later Jherek had almost completed his vast design. It stretched for several miles across a shallow valley through which ran a sparkling river he had named the Thames. Glowing white bridges arched over the water at irregular intervals and the water was a deep, blue-green, to match the roses which climbed the pillars of the bridges. On both sides of the river stood a series of copies of Jones's Kitchen, Coffee Stalls, Prisons, Courts of Law and Hotels. Row upon row, they filled streets of shining marble and gold and quartz and at every intersection was a tall statue, usually of a horse or a hansom cab. It was really very pretty. Jherek had taken the liberty of enlarging the buildings a little, to get variety. Thus a thousand-foot-high Coffee Stall loomed over a five-hundred-foot-high hotel. Farther on, a tall Hotel dwarfed an Old Bailey, and so on.

Jherek was putting the finishing touches on his creation, which he simply called 'London, 1896', when he was hailed by a familiar, languid voice.

'Jherek, you are a genius and this is your masterpiece!'

Mounted upon a great hovering swan, swathed in quilted clothes of the deepest blue, a high collar framing his long, pale face, was Lord Jagged of Canaria, smiling his cleverest, most secret of smiles.

Jherek had been standing on the roof of one of his Prisons. He drifted over and perched on the statue of a hansom close to where Jagged hovered.

'It's a beautiful swan,' said Jherek. 'Have you brought Mrs Underwood with you?'

'So you know what I call her!'

Jherek frowned his puzzlement. 'What?'

'The swan! I thought, gentle Jherek, that you meant the swan. That is what I call the swan, Jherek. Mrs Amelia Underwood. In honour of your friend.'

'Lord Jagged,' said Jherek with a grin. 'You are deceiving me. I know your penchant for manipulation. Remember the world you built, which you peopled with microscopic warriors? This time you have been playing with love, with destiny—with the people you know. You encouraged me to pursue Mrs Amelia Underwood. And most of the details of the rest of that scheme were supplied by you— though you made me believe they were my ideas. I am sure you helped My Lady Charlotina concoct her vengeance. You might even have had something to do with my safe arrival in 1896. Further, it's possible you abducted Mrs Underwood and brought her to our age in the first place.'

Lord Jagged was laughing. He sent the great swan circling around the tallest buildings. He dived and he climbed and all the time he laughed. 'Jherek! You are intelligent! You *are*—you *are* the best of us!'

'But where is Mrs Amelia Underwood now, Lord Jagged?' Jherek Carnelian called, following after his friend, his pale grey suit (with the orange arrows) flapping as he moved through the air. 'I thought you sent a message that you were bringing her back with you!'

'I? A message? No.'

'Then where is she?'

'Why, in Bromley, I suppose. In Kent. In England. In 1896.'

'Oh, Lord Jagged, you are *cruel!*'

'To a degree.' Lord Jagged guided the swan back to where Jherek sat on the head of the statue which, in turn, rested its feet on the dome of the Old Bailey. It was an odd statue—blindfolded, with a sword in one hand and a set of golden scales in the other. 'But did you not learn anything from your sojourn in the past, Jherek?'

'I experienced something, Lord Jagged, but I am not sure I *learned* anything.'

'Well, that is the best way to learn, I think.' Lord Jagged smiled again.

'It was you—the Lord Chief Justice—wasn't it?' Jherek said.

The smile broadened.

'You must get Mrs Amelia Underwood back for me, Lord Jagged,' Jherek told him. 'If only so that she may see this.' He spread both his hands.

'The Morphail Effect,' said Lord Jagged. 'It is an indisputable fact. Brannart says so.'

'You know more.'

'I am flattered. Have you heard, by the by, what became of Mongrove and Yusharisp, the alien?'

'I have been busy. I've heard no gossip at all.'

'They succeeded in building a spaceship and have left together to spread Yusharisp's message throughout the universe.'

'So Mongrove has left us.' Jherek felt sad at hearing this news. 'He will tire of the mission. He will return.'

'I hope so.'

'And your mother, the Iron Orchid. Her liaison with Werther de Goethe is ended, I hear. She took up with the Duke of Queens, who had virtually retired from the world, and they are planning a party together. She will be the guiding spirit, so it should be successful.'

'I am glad,' said Jherek. 'I think I will go to see her soon.'

'Do. She loves you. We all love you, Jherek.'

'And I love Mrs Amelia Underwood,' said Jherek meaningly. 'Will I see her again, Lord Jagged?'

Lord Jagged patted the neck of his graceful swan. The bird began to flap away towards the East.

'Will I?' cried Jherek insistently.

And Lord Jagged called back over his shoulder: 'Doubtless you will. Much can happen yet. After all there are at least a thousand years before the End of Time!'

The white swan soared higher into the blue sky. From its downy back Lord Jagged waved. 'Farewell, my fateful friend. Adieu, my time-tossed leaf, my thief, my grief, my toy! Jherek, my joy, good-bye!'

And Jherek saw the white swan turn its long neck once to look at him from enigmatic black eyes before it disappeared behind a single cloud which drifted in that bland, blind sky.

Dressed in various shades of pale green, the Iron Orchid and her son lay upon a lawn of deeper green which swept gently down to a viridian lake. It was late afternoon and a warm breeze blew.

Between the Iron Orchid and her slender son lay a cloth of greenish-gold and on this were jade plates bearing the remains of their picnic. There were green apples, green grapes and artichoke hearts; there was asparagus, lettuce, cucumber and watercress; little melons, celery and avocados, vine leaves and pears, and, at one corner of the cloth, there stared a radish.

The Iron Orchid's emerald lips opened slightly as she reached for an unpeeled almond. Jherek had been telling her of his adventures at the Dawn of Time. She had been fascinated but not altogether comprehending.

'And did you find out the meaning of "virtue", my bones?' She hesitated over the almond and now considered a cucumber.

He sighed. 'I must admit I am not sure. But I think it might have had something to do with "corruption".' He laughed and stretched his limbs upon the cool grass. 'One thing leads to another, mother.'

'How do you mean, my love, "corruption"?'

'It has something to do with not being in control of your own decisions, I think. Which in turn has something to do with the environment in which you choose to live—if you have a choice at all. Perhaps when Mrs Amelia Underwood returns she will be able to help me.'

'She will return here?' With a gesture of abandonment the Iron Orchid let her fingers fall upon the radish. She popped it into her mouth.

'I am certain of it,' he said.

146

'And then you will be happy!'

He looked at her in mild surprise. 'How do you mean, mother, "happy"?'

The end of the first volume